Children of Morwena

By
Helene Smith

Dedication

For my grandchildren and their children

In memory of Eileen Lee
And my daughter,
Marais

Also, by Helene Smith

Sitting astride K'un on the crest of a high hill, I was filled with anguish. Below me three rivers glinted like frosted spider webs against the darkness of the land. Slowly, red light from the rising sun spread to where the three rivers became one broad stream.

'These waters will go on flowing whatever becomes of us,' I murmured, 'Oh, Andre, where are you and where is Bonnie?'

1

A Family

The Taree surged ahead of us. Dad leapt from port to starboard, pulling lines, shouting orders, 'Leila! Andre!' We jumped to it while Mum steered Vesta through the channel to the open sea. The swell lifted us and we slid over the hump.

High-tech wars and a major shift in thinking had changed the way we lived but with a sail, the sea and the wind, we might have been any family at any time in history.

'Slow down Rolf, it isn't a race.' Mum had Bonnie straddled across her back and she wanted peace. But to Dad it was a race...between brothers. Tough with fierce blue eyes, he grinned at Andre and me.

'Go boat! Go!' I clutched the rail, my body tilted towards the rush of water.

'We're gaining on them,' Dad shouted.

'Hey Andre, look at Huldah and Tristan!' I was in such a tizz I nearly fell overboard. On board the Taree, our cousins and uncle struggled to control their mainsail. It billowed and then flapped crazily. It was enough. The Vesta tacked at a safe 45-degree angle to the wind, easily overtaking the Taree.

'Huldah! Tristan! See you this time never!' I made a V with my arms and got rude finger signs. Tristan grinned. Blonde and sun-tanned, he yelled above the wind, 'Leila, see you in Morwena to-night.'

I sang and shimmied. We were off to sell oils and garden pro-duce to traders along the waterways of Morwena. The raggedy old city had taken a battering when Norland zapped us. But that hap-pened when Mum and Dad were young like us. Tonight, there was money to spare and fun for us kids.

For the rest of the year we lived quietly on the flood plains of the Tanjin River on the outskirts of Morwena. Andre and I worked with Mum and Dad or spent time with friends on the river. We were Hardies with our own proud traditions. Mum taught us the laws and languages of our land. She showed us how to write and keep our stories and songs on a microchip no bigger than a pin head.

Mum told us the myths of our land. About her people who came across the sea on a magic rope and my father's people who were washed up on this shore – a gift to this land from their mother, Morwena – the wave. It was the name given to our city in her honour.

Dad was the one who took us outside our village. He talked to us about the things that had happened to shape our lives, good and bad. About the high-tech wars of the past, about rising seas and the ozone scare. Through Dad we met people like the mud-skippers who lived in the foulest places between drowned cities. You'd see them mucking through half-submerged mansions look-ing for something useful to sell. They were the refugees from the old world, Dad said.

But for us, except for the seasons our lives were unchanging – our trip to the city centre, the highlight of our year.

'Andre, can you wait?' I wanted action.

'I can wait…little sister.' My brother tapped out a beat on the rail with his fingers.

'Andre, tighten that line,' Dad yelled.

'I'll do it, Dad.' I took up the slack and Dad gave me a thumbs-up sign. A sour-grapes grin from Andre. He tugged my hair and I tried to get him back. We chased each other round the deck but soon our jealous squabble turned to laughter.

Dusky-skinned like Mum, Bonnie peeped at us, her dark eyes dancing. Mum put her down and she ran to us, lifting chubby arms. We both rushed to pick her up.

'Come Bihbi,' I took in the clean, nut-like smell of her head as I swung her onto my skinny hip.

'Shake, shake,' she demanded.

'We'll give you a shake, Bihbi.' Andre took her upper body. I took her feet and between us we tossed her in the air while chanting, 'A- shake, a-shake, a-one, a-two, a-three!'

'Enough,' Mum called. 'You'll make her sick.'

We put Bonnie down and she took a few dizzy steps, spewed a curdle of milk and then ran. When Andre grabbed her, she protested, 'No! Bonnie not fall.' She yelled and bawled to be free until Andre put her on his shoulders and took her forward. We stood with our faces to the wind.

'Is she smiling?' Andre asked. The whole day glittered with shaken light.

'Not really smiling but I know she likes it.'

Bonnie clutched Andre's head with both hands, her dark eyes closed against the wind as our sailboat cut through the water. A moment to remember always. The mainsail luffed. I crossed my fingers and counted the family members. My secret safeguard against disaster.

2

A City

At the end of the day the Vesta and Taree came together. We nosed our way past houseboats, barges and sails, into the heart of the city. In times past, channels had been cut, crisscross, into the coastal plain of Westland. With the boats docked, Andre and I gaped at the scene. So different from our own small village.

On either side of narrow waterways, a honeycomb of living pads overflowed with refugees from war and famine. On these streets people of every race came together where they ate, slept, lived. I watched a fat grandmother string wet clothes across her balcony. She yelled at a hawker on the street below. His illegal char-burner billowed pollution, but he went on calling out to passers-by, 'Want to buy fried pigeon cheap? Only five copper buks.'

Other hawkers pushed their carts along the pavement screaming for people to buy. Traders from all over Westland had come together for the summer markets.

'In the old days these streets were packed with all kinds of vehicles,' Dad said. 'Until they were banned you went everywhere by car.'

Andre and I grinned at each other. We waited for him to tell us about a time before the wars, when people rode on giant air-trains

4

and the rest.

'Oh yeah, Dad.' We were tired of hearing about the old days. Since the ban on nuclear power and the ozone scare, you took a solar taxi or even an animo-cart. Rich people hired hydro-fuelled zip-cars or took a fast-moving electric train or coach. But they were not for us. I bounced on my own strong feet. If I wanted to go places I had to walk or go by sail.

A whiff of mixed-up food smells…a jangle of sound. Above the din I made out the steady beat of a snare drum.

'That's Zara,' Andre said quietly.

'Who is she?' Dad asked.

'She's the drummer from our village,' I said. 'She's busking in the mall.'

Dad muttered, 'A girl alone and so young, busking in the city like that, I don't like it.'

Andre and I rolled our eyes. 'Oh Dad,' we both sighed, yet I knew I wasn't brave enough to do the things Zara did. City bred, with different ways she had caused a stir among us kids when she came to live with her father in our village. I caught a glimpse of her bending over her drum, glossy black hair cut close to her neat little head. Her quick hands flashed. We couldn't keep our eyes off her.

The crowd thinned. A group of kids bunched up together in the mosh pit near the buskers. Their bodies moved as one. They chanted as one, their voices gliding along with the twang of guitars and beat of the drum.

'Can we go now, Mum? Can we go and see?' My heart beat a little faster.

'Wait for your cousins,' Mum said.

Within minutes Huldah and Tristan came by with hair slicked down, and pants bleached to whiteness like ours

'You're a hunky pair tonight,' I said.

Embarrassed, Huldah pulled a vinegar face and then hurried

us along with an impatient, 'Well? Are you coming?'

'Yes, sweet cousin.' I grinned. 'But first I have to put on my swish new hat.'

Mum had made the hat by hand from a precious ream of cloth, using tiny stitches, criss-cross neat. It felt like feather strokes on my forehead. Blue-green, a tinge of gold, the hat showed off my newly trimmed shoulder-length hair.

'It makes your eyes as green as the sea,' Mum said with a smile.

'Wild with your dark skin,' said Tristan.

A brotherly pinch on the arm from Andre. He reminded me not to lose it but I knew he approved too and even Huldah murmured, 'yes!'

Dad fussed around, telling us to stick to the central mall and to lookout for one another. 'Mind who you speak to,' he warned.

You wouldn't dare speak with a ferl. They were homeless kids, or streeks as they were sometimes called, the ones who'd gone wild. You found them in the back alleys of the city. Sometimes the government blitzed them. They were nabbed by the kops. Thrown out of town. People said they lived in hand-dug caves in the hills above Morwena.

Ferls, streeks, they didn't seem real to me. I blew on Bonnie's fat cheek and gave Mum and Dad a hug. It was my first time out with the older kids. We pushed through the crowded mall, Andre on one side of me, Huldah and Tristan on the other. Only Emily and Jacob are missing I thought. My two best friends.

A solar taxi nudged right up to us and we stood aside.

'We ought to put our buks together and have a ride, Tristan said.

Huldah raised an eyebrow, 'Spend all our buks in one hit and then what?' But Tristan's eyes were everywhere. 'Sugarcane…roasted yams…and look over there, you can take a pot shot and win a prize.' He rushed from one thing to another and then sprinted away from us.

'The scatterwit!' Huldah scowled. 'He'll be lost and Grandma's sure to blame me. Ever since Mum died he's been her little pet.'

We all shouted, 'Tristan!'

A fast-moving coach beeped us. We jumped out of the way and then an animo-cart laden with techno scrap blocked us. 'Haya Up!' cried the driver and the hybrid cow lumbered past us.

'Where is he?' Huldah freaked out as we darted between trading carts looking for Tristan. 'He'll get himself bashed by a ferl.'

'Let's stand with our backs to each other and look for him.' I scanned the mall. Crowds of people went by. Families, traders, village kids like us dressed up in their best, along with rejects of every kind.

'Got a copper-buk for a night-scrounger?' A skinny old woman rattled her tin.

A boy of about sixteen with long matted hair and queer hungry eyes slid past us.

'There's a ferl,' Andre whispered.

I turned away from the grizzled face and then I spotted Tristan and my heart lifted.

'Hey guys, you missed out on the jugglers and the clown!' His pockets and his hands were full. 'Look I got food and knick-knacks for Gran and everything…cheap as cheap.'

'I know your idea of cheap,' Huldah muttered. 'Now you've spent your buks on a lot of rubbish, Grandma will expect me to share with you.'

'Give me a break,' Tristan groaned. 'Look, there's Zara and she's playing her drum. Let's go and see her.' Tristan dragged us along with him and Huldah grumbled but as we approached the buskers, his face smoothed out. He slicked back his hair, his gaze on Zara.

'Let's mosh.' Tristan grinned, taking my arm on one side and Andre's on the other. I grabbed Huldah's arm and the four of us bunched up together close to the buskers.

The drummer girl's peat-coloured eyes moved from Andre to Huldah and back to Andre. Her lips curved in a smile. A glimpse of white teeth. We clapped and cheered the musicians. When it was over we stayed on to talk to Zara.

'You ought to join our outfit,' Tristan told her.

'Didn't know you had one,' said Zara, her eyes full of mischief.

'We haven't yet, but we could easily get together and make one. I play pipes and Huldah plays lip-music.' Tristan leaned over and grabbed the instrument out of Huldah's pocket brushing it lightly over his mouth.

Huldah grabbed it back, glaring at his brother, but Tristan went on. 'Leila can shimmy and use shakers. Then we have Andre. He plays guitar, but he has a voice.'

'Then he can be the singer,' said Zara, smiling.

It was like watching cloth being woven. Zara and Andre together with Huldah looking on. The dreamy look in Andre's eyes made me think there was already a song about the girl and her drum spinning away in his head.

'Don't you feel it?' I whispered to Tristan.

He laughed. 'What do you mean…feel what?'

'I don't know. Nothing,' I replied, yet I was sure Huldah understood.

He turned away as if he couldn't bear to watch. A few quiet words to Tristan, 'Stay with Andre until I get back. I'm going to look at the stalls.'

I watched him leaving and felt a strange ache in my middle. 'Huldah, wait,' I called. 'I'll come with you.'

We wondered around the stalls, boggle-eyed from all we saw. Among rows of sparkling trinkets, I pointed out some earrings, a friendship pair. They were perfect for Emily and me to share.

'Jacob asked me to buy him a paring knife,' Huldah said. 'He wanted to pay me to bargain for it.'

'The dagwit.' I said. 'As if you'd charge a friend for that.'

'Jacob doesn't look on me as a friend,' he said. 'None of the kids do.'

The hawker pulled on Huldah's arm. 'Sir…for a silver buk you can buy your girlfriend a crystal.'

'You heard the man.' I grinned at Huldah.

Huldah held the earrings I had chosen between his fingertips. 'They look like tear-drops,' he said, softly and then brightened. 'Will I bargain for them?'

I nodded. 'Go for it, Huldah. Nobody bargains like you.'

I soon had the two shining crystals in my bag and we made for the food stalls where we ate greasy kelp burgers with our fingers. Out of the corner of my eye I saw the ferl on the edge of the crowd, slipping between trading carts. I avoided him as he came close. At the same time, I felt his gaze flicking over me…my leather shoes…my pretty hat.

'Now for Jacob's knife,' Huldah said.

I turned my back on the ferl, trying to concentrate on the knives. There were so many to choose from. Huldah tested one with his thumb. 'Rubbish!' He tested another one. 'Now here's a goody for you. Just feel that.'

'No, Huldah, I don't want to…get it away from me.' I couldn't stand the look of it.

'What's wrong with you, Leila? It's only a paring knife.' Huldah gave up on me. 'I'll trade.' His eyes glinted from the fun of it but there was something steely about his trading. The man backed down.

'Two silver buks then,' he muttered, while Huldah turned to me with a rare wide smile.

'Ready to go home now?'

I brushed away a feeling of uneasiness. 'Huldah! I haven't spent all my buks.' I took my purse out of my bag and waved it at him, laughing. 'I don't want to take any of it home with me!'

A flicker of movement behind me, the strong smell of un-washed body and then steely fingers ripped the purse from my fingers.

Huldah shouted, 'Thief.'

Two kops appeared. My purse flew into the crowd and a gang of streeks scrambled after it. For a second, forever, the ferl's eyes bore into mine and then the kop's baton came down on him. Blood gushed from a wound on his head.

'I'll get you, girl…I'll get you for this,' he screamed.

I was shocked by the violence of the kop, at the gushing wound, at the hatred I saw in the ferl's eyes. A few people stopped to stare but within minutes the boy's voice was swallowed by the tramp of feet, the hubbub of the city.

Politely, the same kop came back to ask me, 'Do you want to stay while we look for your purse, Miss?'

'No. No.' I couldn't meet his eyes. I wanted to go home. Home to Mum and Dad and Bonnie.

3

A Ship

We left the city next day to trawl for fish in the open sea and then anchored for the night. It was so quiet on deck with just Andre and me. We were looking out for a ship Dad had seen earlier. You could hear the rolling whoosh of waves on a distant shore. A cool wind touched my face.

'Say hello to Emily.' I imagined this same wind touching my friend's face. 'Tomorrow we're coming home.'

Home to our land. I was like Mum. I loved to have my hands in the earth planting things. The black soil of the flood plain had a voice as strong as the sea and I was part of it. If you have land you live, Mum always said. A collector of seeds, she kept them in a dillybag tied to her waist the way others carried their gold.

As it grew darker, I drew a little closer to Andre. We heard a low rumble and then the sailboat lifted and rocked beneath us.

'Wow…it's a high-tech battleship.' Andre let out his breath. 'I thought they were banned.'

We stared at the dimly lit vessel sliding into the night. I shivered, wanting the warmth and clutter of the galley. Within minutes Dad called us and we raced each other to be first inside.

Laughing, Andre gave me a gentle shove and ran while I was

left in the dark with my fears. A creature with cold sea fingers had brushed against me. I hurried below deck where Andre and Dad were already discussing the ship and what it might be.

'Andre, you cheated!' I yelled, relieved to be in the light.

'Don't start fighting you two,' Mum warned. She had an armful of wriggling child. 'Andre, you help Dad with dinner while Leila helps me.'

After we had bathed Bonnie, she threw herself at us, glowing and clean, to be tickled and held and petted. I laughed as she put her head to my chest to see if I had a beating heart like hers. She touched my lips to feel my breath on her fingers.

At last she grew sleepy though she went on smiling until her eyes closed. Mum was singing the same song she sang to Andre and me when we were young: Sweet and low, wind of the western sea…. We tucked Bonnie into the bunk next to mine, covering her with her quilt. It had been hand painted with yellow ducks, green grass, and a clear blue sky. A little girl's quilt.

Afterwards I said, 'Can we stay here for a minute, Mum?' A moment warm and safe.

'Happy, Leila?'

I couldn't bring myself to speak. There were things I didn't understand. Shadows I hadn't seen before.

With her arms around me, Mum drew me to the porthole. 'Everything is okay. Look at the spread of lights across Morwena. Aren't they pretty?'

I peeped at the lights and then drew in my breath as everything went black.

'It's nothing. Only a blackout,' Mum said. 'Lucky we have our own lights.'

4

A River

As the weeks passed we heard whispers. A man from Norland's banned Technocrat Party had been voted in as Top Controller. He'd torn up agreements reached by the Union of All Nations. The UAN as we called it was our security. It had banned all weapons of war and declared the world a peace zone.

Everyone wanted to know what this meant for Westland. 'Nothing,' said officials at our government info-centres. Vesrigo, our trading partner won't have it. The UAN won't have it. Voice of World reflects the wishes of the people. We are all tired of settling disputes with mass murder in the name of war. Voice of World won't have it.

Messages in our inboxes told us something else:

Vesrigo and Norland both want world dominance.

Norland says Westland is allowing Vesrigo to use it as a base to infiltrate Norland's markets. Westland should be punished.

Norland is disputing the UAN decision to give Westland its statehood at all. It used to be part of Norland.

Norland wants to show muscle. The Technocrats have a Killer and are chafing at the bit to use it. Vesrigo's ally will be hit....

'Dad,' I worried. 'These messages scare me...they reckon we'll be zapped.'

'Don't believe this rubbish,' he said.

That same day an old mudskipper tried to sell him an info-chip. 'It's all about Norland's Killer. You can have it for a hydro-cell.'

Dad laughed in his face. 'I give you a hydro-cell and my family will be cold next winter. Now get out of here and stop scaring my kids.'

The worry of it slid off me. Whatever happens, Dad will take care of us, I thought. From that time, each day came like a page of a book to be read. While Mum worked with Dad, I took care of Bonnie. I watched how she lifted her hands when she saw sunlight stream through a window.

She cried out, 'Dold!' Her word for gold. Bonnie could find it anywhere. In the eye of a turtle or the mottled skin of a frog. We looked for reflections in shiny things. The river was best – you could see a sky in there, a huge white dome.

One day while we all worked in the garden, Bonnie ran to the river alone but Dad and I found her before she could slip into the dome – the upside-down sky. I was the first to get to her and I held her close to me, my heart thumping with fear.

'Here, let me take her,' Dad said, and she rode home high in his arms.

Andre changed that summer. In the mornings you would see him planting rows of oil tree seedlings, his hands moving like a machine, but you could tell he wanted to be out of there. His real life was music. He dreamed of making songs for the Voice of World talent scouts.

Along with our cousins and Zara, he went busking in our village streets. You would hear him singing:

Drummer girl…drummer girl…why can't you see me? Drummer girl…drummer girl…you're drivin' me crazy…. That song was driving me crazy. I couldn't help singing along with him and the tune stayed in my head for days

I saw Zara and Andre together one day. They weren't touching, but it made me think of water and water. Put a tiny drop of it on a coin and another drop near and you would see the pull. That night I lay in my bunk wondering if they ever did more than kiss. I traced the curve of my cheekbones with my fingertips...my throat...my lips.

Without our knowing it, time slipped through our fingers like sand. In the afternoons we village kids spent hours by the river. We swam, dived and leapt into the water from a rope swing that dangled from the stout limb of a river gum. We piled onto a wooden raft which sagged under the weight of so many of us. We laughed and screeched until the sun went down and the air whistled with the sound of wings as the water birds flew home to roost.

My best friend Emily and I wore our matching crystal earrings night and day.

'Emily!' the boys would cry.

They all wanted Emily. She moved with a flash of arms and legs, her plait of fair hair bobbing around her shoulders. Wherever Emily went, there was laughter. She would dive into the water, chasing Tristan.

'Don't you think he's a babe?' she whispered.

'He's my cousin and Mum says in our family a cousin can't be a babe. How about Jacob?'

'He's my brother, you scatterwit.'

'But not mine.' I liked Jacob's calm face and clear eyes and the way he waited for the right moment to speak.

'Do you mind?' Jacob asked.

For the first time in my life I felt shy with him but I made room for him and we sat on my towel on the river bank watching Emily and Tristan diving in the shallows like a pair of seal pups.

'I wish...I was like Emily.' My lips parted in a smile.

'Don't. Don't even think of it.' Jacob said. 'You're...Leila Kieva...that's enough. Want to swim out to the raft with me?'

At the end of the day on the river my limbs were waterweed. I sprawled on the sandbank near Emily, too tired to lift my head. I listened while she told me her every passing thought. Emily loved the colour purple. Hated talk of death and gloomy things. Always slept with a lighted candle by her side.

'The dark makes my skin crawl,' she admitted.

Emily had a friend named Colly whose family had made a fortune in Norland. They were coming back to live in our village because they no longer felt welcome there.

I drifted off to sleep hearing about Colly: her big boobies, her gorgeous Norlander boyfriend and her fast metal sail. I imagined her with her golden-skinned boy, superhuman and fabulous, riding waves as smoothly as a bird in flight.

When I woke, the night was black and Emily was yelling, 'My eyes! I can't see! I can't see!'

'Of course, you can't see. We've been asleep and its dark!'

'Oh...oh...I had a bad dream.' Emily laughed but her breath came out, raspy and quick.

'Look, here's Mum come to find us,' I said.

'Leila! Emily!' Mum held up her lantern to show us the way, scolding us for staying out so late. We scrambled to our feet and with a quick glance over her shoulder, Emily rushed to be in front of me. Playfully we struggled to be the one close to Mum, wanting to feel the brush of her long hair, her safe warmth. But there was something precious about Emily that made me stand back. I slipped in next to my friend and with arms round each other, we walked home, singing all the way, the glow of the lantern leaping before us.

5

The Rushing Tide

When Colly came to our village everything changed. Our streets were packed with newcomers from Norland. Some had spoken out against the Top Controller. Others had come because they believed they had a right to be here. Westland and Norland are one state, they claimed. The creation of a separate state was cooked up by Vesrigo after the wars and the UAN fell for it.

Wealthy newcomers took over businesses. They had different ways. At the info-centre a Norlander checked and rechecked my pass as though I hadn't a right to be there. She disappeared with it behind a screen and I heard her say, 'Check this girl's records please, Stefan. I'm cracking down on unschooled Hardies taking up spaces in here. If she hasn't passed her A-level info-com test, send her away.'

Unschooled Hardies? Insulted, I bit my lip yet somehow, I understood why a woman like her might say such a thing. Mum and Dad worked hard to give Andre and me time to learn a written language but not all of my friends' parents were like mine.

I thought of Emily who could barely read, and Jacob who had struggled to master the A-level test without any help or encouragement. Yet give Emily a zip-needle, some thread and a piece of cloth and she could make anything, while Jacob was wanted everywhere for what he knew about herbal medicines, massage and healing.

Mum always said we Hardies were as tough as she-oaks, the trees you found growing in brackish swamps or on high arid plains where no other tree could grow. I was proud of my heritage and ready to face this Stefan whoever he was. My Hardie blood was up.

'Why would a girl like you want an A-level port?'

My anger dissolved when I saw a boy with laughing eyes and a quirky grin. 'I can't do anything about her but I can show you our new info-machine.'

I shook my head. 'That would cost more buks than I have.'

'Then you can use my special pass.'

We sat together at the slick machine.

'What would you like?' Stefan's keen eyes searched my face.

'The world,' I said, smiling.

'Impossible,' he said, 'but I can show you what I think of it right now.'

I nodded and he began his creation, using nothing but images and colour. Fiery oranges and pulsing reds and then something soft and cool. A stream of words came to mind: water, earth, day, night, velvet, petal, cup, bowl, bread, love. And then suddenly a spreading darkness. With a flick of the controls Stefan made a map. I knew my history too and I knew what he was saying. It was a world in ruin after war. Populations reduced. Devastation.

'It won't happen again, Stefan. You're being too dark.' I tapped out my own images: green for growth, yellow for sunlight and health. I shaped a garden. It was Andre and Bonnie and me. It was Mum and Dad. Their hard work and love. It was a way of life that to me was unshakable.

I looked at Stefan defiantly but his fingers were busy spoiling my picture, creating small monsters with bulging bellies and gaping mouths. One with a white mane of hair pranced across a shining screen, preening himself.

'He's talking about old boundaries,' Stefan began.

'The UAN won't let him stir up trouble.'

'He's got the Technocrats behind him.'

'The Technocrats are dead.'

'And he's got GRIM.'

Embarrassed I shrugged my shoulders, too vain to admit I knew little about GRIM. They were a fraternity of criminals as strange and distant as a rogue asteroid from space.

'You're living in dreamland, Leila. If Norland and Vesrigo come to blows, nobody will be safe from GRIM.' Stefan's face tightened. A muscle pulsed in his temple.

'I wish you hadn't told me this, Stefan,' I whispered.

For a moment the comforting pressure of his hand was there on my wrist and we stared at one another like two people stranded in a flood. I'd known as soon as I saw him – he was Colly's babe, the golden-skinned boy, a rider of waves. I heard the buzz of machines and then the hushed library silence broken by the sound of girls' laughter.

'Leila! What are you doing here?' Emily started in surprise. 'Colly and I came to find Stefan. He's coming out on the sail with us…I see you've already met him.'

Stefan coloured faintly. His palm brushed my arm as it fell from my wrist. We stood awkwardly until he found voice enough to introduce me to Colly – a girl with dark eyes and a red lipstick smile.

This was the meeting Emily and I had dreamed about, when two best friends became three. For a second Colly's eyes narrowed with instant dislike and then she was smiling. 'Oh Stefan, the manager told me I'd find you here. You've worked overtime. Emily and I have been waiting.'

Colly's fast metal sail was the sleekest craft any of us village kids had ever seen. Every day you would see her with Stefan and

Emily and the chosen ones. They flashed along the waterways, following the Tanjin River until it disappeared into the purple-tinted blue.

While she made her choice for the day, Colly's eyes had a way of passing through me as though I were not visible. Andre, Zara, Huldah and Tristan – each one tried the sail. Only Jacob seemed to notice I was never included and when Colly called out, 'Jacob, you're next,' he said, 'No, I don't think so.'

Colly's face reddened with quick anger and then she was all smiles again. 'Oh…please yourself, Jacob. I'll be faster without you.' Deftly, she turned away from the shore, becoming one with her craft. Watching her, I almost felt the water and wind parting for her.

I didn't speak to Stefan again. No more than a few words. He'd been in trouble at work for allowing me to use the new info-machine and for being over friendly with a client. This I learned from Emily. Sometimes he looked at me when he thought I wasn't watching or he would look at me when I was watching and for a moment we shared something…a kind of knowledge that neither of us really wanted. But mostly he was with Colly, clowning around, laughing, riding the waves and she would rest her hand on his bare shoulder so naturally.

Emily began to wear red lipstick. Emily began to sound like Colly. Wherever I went I would hear Colly's clear ringing voice and Emily's laughter.

Emily and I had an understanding. Each year we would meet at a given time to attend the summer festival together but when I called for her, Jacob told me she had already gone with Colly and Stefan.

'Didn't she think to let me know?' I asked.

It had been happening a lot lately. Jacob shook his head. He looked at me with soft eyes but there was nothing he could do or say to take away the hurt. A friendship that had made the days so bright had suddenly fallen away. I went to the river alone. The kids had scuffed up the sand. A gusting wind rippled through the river gums and then slowed to a winnow and sigh in the Sheoaks. The tide rushed in. Fingers of water filled the bumps and hollows of a footprint. I imagined this place after I'd gone. No footprints, no voices.

6

Shifting Sands

If it had to happen then you should be able to choose a time. But there is no right time for disaster. No way of seeing it all. You remember bits. A scene, a smell, a feeling comes back to haunt you.

We'd gone by sail across the estuary to the beach. With fishing rods in their hands, Mum and Dad stand as still as statues. Bonnie holds a shell to her ear and smiles. Andre lies flat on his back to watch the flight of a sea eagle.

I run into the sea to catch a wave, flinging myself into an icy swirl of foam.

'Morwena!' I cry over the sea's roar. How I loved my homeland. Its sea and its soil. I needed both.

I swim across the current, then body-surf the waves, one after another, until, famished I run to find a picnic basket overflowing with yeasty-bread, cheese, melons and berries from the garden.

The day unfolded.

Wandering along the beach, I bent down to pick up a nautilus shell thrown up by the tide when I heard the kop siren's first wail. It warned of the single event that would rob us of our childhood and everything we knew.

I called to Andre, who was sitting on a rock, looking out to sea. There was something about the droop of his shoulders that went to my heart. I ran towards him, wanting to protect him from hurt while telling myself, I mustn't be worried. We are all okay. The kop siren has nothing to do with us.

'Don't look so scared.' Andre had come to meet me. 'The safety people must be staging an emergency training session.'

I stood there feeling foolish. 'You should have come for a swim.' It was all I could think to say. I shivered.

'Oh yeah. Lovely day for a swim.'

We each gave a forced kind of laugh but uneasiness pricked me. Andre's brows crinkled into worry lines. We walked towards our picnic spot.

'Where's Bonnie?' Andre started to run.

'Where is Bonnie? I can't see her.'

Mum and Dad were picking up our things but there was no sign of Bonnie. Instant fear pushed at my throat. Bonnie...where are you, Bihbi? I ran with a dreamlike illusion that I was making no headway, as if the sands beneath me were shifting too.

I watched Andre streak ahead and he soon turned to me with a relieved grin. 'Look at her. She's still in the pool we made for her. With the sand built up around her we couldn't see her.'

'Watch out! Look at that wave,' Dad yelled.

Mum snatched Bonnie up as the hungry surf snapped at the sand. Even Dad looked tiny against the huge black waves. Beyond the sound of the surf, kop sirens screamed.

It was the last time our family would ever be together again in this way. This was no fake disaster. Back at home, our village kop told us the truth, though Dad seemed to know without being told. 'It's the madman from Norland. He's letting the Technocrats loose.'

The kop nodded. 'They're razing our cities. Morwena will be hit hardest.'

With wide eyes, Andre and I stared at the kop while he told us to get ready for an evacuation. Each person would need sleeping gear, clothes, and food. No time to waste.

'My people came from the north,' Mum said, bitterly. 'Our families have been mixing for generations and now this.'

'They won't even dirty their hands with our blood,' Dad said, softly. 'This is no raid. They plan to use the Killer.'

The kop's voice was strangely flat. 'Nobody knows how bad it will be. They're boasting it's a clean device with no fallout but we expect earth tremors brought on by a rupture in the sea floor. There'll be a killer wave.'

Morwena, the wave. The myth of my father's people ran through my mind like a theme song. Foolishly, I whispered, 'You can't destroy what was created in your name.'

'What's the point of the Union of All Nations or Voice of World,' Mum said. 'They were created to stop such carnage.'

I looked at Dad and realised he and Mum knew more than they ever told us. They had even prepared for such an emergency.

'You should have told us,' I cried, but I thought, what a blind fool I'd been. I should have known. Stefan tried to warn me and I chose not to listen.

Dad will take care of us. That is what I believed in my childish heart but Dad was only one man. No match for blind Technocrats and a Top Controller with murder in his heart. For the first time in my life I saw my father's hand shaking. I saw fear in his eyes but he held us three kids and Mum in the circle of his arms until Mum reminded him gently, 'There are things to be done, Rolf, and things to be left undone.'

We villagers were taken to the central station by coach but already hundreds were leaving the city by zip-car, solar plane or coach, all reserved for those who could pay. We'd have to rely on trains and the slower steam-driven buses. At the central pad, thousands of people spilled into the streets. A woman spoke through the com system in a deadpan voice. Passengers would be taken to camps set up by emergency workers. Train A would go to Camp A. Train B to Camp B and so on.

Words went back and forth. Rumours spread like wildfire.

'There won't be enough places on the trains.'

'They're asking for money.'

'They'll take anything – hydro-cells, medicines, gem stones, healing oils, gold buks, you name it.'

Tears stream down a man's face. 'They'll make room for my wife and kids but not my old father.'

A child screams. Time running out. A woman's cry, 'You expect me to send my kids away without me?'

A red faced official says, 'I've sent my kids ahead of me. Is that so stupid? This train will be back…keep in line there…next one please.'

A man in a uniform talks to himself. A kop or a transport official. 'There are too many people and not enough trains or coaches. There's no way we can get all these people out of Morwena in time.'

I clung to Dad and he saved me from being swept along by a human tide. With his strong back against a panicking mob, he was able to speak with an official from Train B, handing over a small bag of gold-buks.

'We'll take the girl.' The man unlocked a steel mesh guard to let me through. 'You miss out on this trip, Mister.'

A quick hug from Dad. I got a whiff of his old fishing cape, felt the prickle of his unshaven face against mine.

'Don't worry. This train will come back for us. We'll meet you at Camp B.'

Mum tried to reach me but was pushed away by a throng of people. My gaze rushed to hers over the distance. She called out, 'Seeds. I've put my dilly-bag of seeds in the flap of your backpack. Don't trade with them. Keep them for our land.'

'Yes!' A silent goodbye past between us. In her arms, Bonnie peeped out from her feather quilt. Goodbye little sister. Goodbye my Bihbi.

I squeezed into a padded space meant for luggage with my own swag cushioning my back. Nearby a woman and her three children talked and laughed as if they were going on a holiday.

On the opposite bank, Train A slid along the railing and I spotted Andre running beside it. Zara, Huldah and Tristan had jammed the door open and were screaming. 'Andre, jump! Jump now!' Though burdened with backpack and guitar, my brother flung himself at the open door to safety.

A flash of carriages and his train flicked past. Hundreds of people rushed to take up the space left by its passengers. As my own train moved out I caught a last glimpse of the city of Morwena.

7

A Cave

When Norland's Killer penetrated the earth's crust, Westland shuddered with sound and aftershocks. Earth tremors spread outwards one after another. A hot spot in the sea's floor ruptured. A great wave washed over the city of Morwena.

I knew none of this, only a sense of my world, shaken by a drunken fist. My train, zigzagging round a far-off mountain range east of the city, buckled. Jumping the rails, it flicked off its tail like a terrified lizard, the head section gutted by fire within minutes. I was on a ride to nowhere. Metal crunched on metal. A woman screamed.

I walked in the dark.

My backpack dragged on my shoulder. Sometimes I crawled on hands and knees to feel my way over the rough ground. Too tired to go on, I lay on the bare ground, slipping into sleep. I dreamed about fire. I dreamed about silence and the woman who screamed.

In the morning there were prickles on my hands and blood on my face. My forehead felt puffed and strange. I have to go home. I have to find Mum and Dad. It was the only thing I could hold in my mind. I walked in a place where lizards sunned themselves on rocks. I walked until I heard the faint wailing of kop sirens and then I vomited on the grass. A boy leaned over me.

'You've been hurt bad,' he said. 'You better come with me. The rescue people have gone away.' We stumbled into a hand-dug trench. Here and there scraps of metal and timber had been placed on top to form a rough shelter.

'Listen!' the boy whispered. 'Earth tremors.' He led me to a place where you could see the roots of trees in the wall.

'Is this a grave?' I asked, dumbly. When the tremors stopped I said to the boy, 'I must go. I must find out what happened to Mum and Dad. I want to go back to Morwena.'

'But there's nothing left,' said the boy.

Brushing him aside, I found a road where people moved in a slow stream. A lady waited near a roadblock which might have led back to the city.

'You can't go past this point.' Her high chirpy voice grated on me but my gaze never left her face as I told her about my missing family.

'If your Mum and Dad were waiting for Train B they never got out…I know because my son works for the rescue people.' The woman's eyes gleamed and her voice rose even higher as if she didn't dare feel anything except the surge of energy that sent her rushing with self-importance from one group of survivors to another with information and words of advice.

'What about my little sister?' I held my breath. No matter how bad it was, I needed to know.

'I don't know about your little sister. At the last, there was no standing room in the coaches. Not even for a child. But mothers were passing their babies through windows to be held by any willing arms to give their little ones a chance at life.'

'Mum would do that for Bonnie. Thank you, oh thank you.' I snatched at the woman's words as a lifeline and I wasn't going to let go.

'If that is the case,' said the woman, 'and you can't be sure it is, there's no way you'd know where she is. She could be in any one of the camps across the country. You ought to take care of yourself first. Get yourself to the nearest camp. They're trying to find foster families to take children like you.'

The woman bustled over to another group of people, while I went on saying, 'Bihbi, Bihbi, I must find you now. I must.' I staggered around like somebody drunk and then the boy who had given me shelter was tugging my arm.

'You're no good in your head just yet. You better come back to my place.'

For days I lived in the half-light of his cave. The boy wiped blood from my face. He gave me bits of food and sips of water. Mostly I slept to dream and dream until I hardly knew what was real. Sometimes I thought I was at home harvesting the corn Mum and I had planted in the rich black soil of Morwena.

Slowly the swelling around my head went down and my chest cleared. I awoke to my life in the aftermath.

Morwena, the wave, I thought, you gave your children to the land, and now you've taken them back again.

I put my hand on Mum's dilly-bag of seeds to make sure they were safely tied to my body. On the ground beside me the cave boy slept with his mouth open until something disturbed him and he was instantly awake. Gently I raised my right knee and then lay still, feigning sleep, I watched him through half closed eyes. He crept towards me and in a flash, he had my left boot undone but as he eased it away from my foot, I brought my right food down on his shoulder and pushed hard.

'They're my boots. Leave them alone!' Shocked with myself, I stood up as he reeled back, rolling over on the ground.

'Aha…ah,' he groaned.

'You were trying to steal my boots!' I screamed. 'Why did you do that?'

'Sodden boots. I don't need 'em.' He turned his back on me

and poked at a hole in the ground. 'Look what I got here and tell me if I need 'em.' He had a big cloth bag in his hand which he up-ended on the ground. Boots and shoes of all kinds tumbled out. Some new, others dirty and worn.

'You stole these, didn't you?' I cried in disgust. This boy lived by himself and he stole things. I wanted to tell somebody about it. I wanted to tell Mum and Dad. But there was no Mum and no Dad to tell.

There's only me and this boy. He's younger than I am. He's dirty and he's a thief. I don't even know his name.

Stupidly, I asked, 'Who are you?'

'I'm called Shoeboy,' he said, sulkily.

It was no kind of name, although I couldn't think of anything better, but I was puzzled by him.

'If you had to take my boots why leave it 'til now?'

'Wasn't fair until now,' he muttered. 'I knew yesterday you was coming good.'

'What else have you taken?' I looked around for my backpack which had been lying on its side near my sleeping-bag. 'My back-pack! You took it, didn't you?'

Shoeboy bristled. 'It weren't me.' He shook his head. 'Honest, it were here last night. I never touched it. I never even looked at it.'

'My hat was in that backpack.' My hat with the lovely mix of colours. Blue, green, a tinge of gold. 'My Mum made it for me,' I sobbed. 'My brother warned me not to lose it.' Until now I hadn't wanted to cry. I hadn't cried. I hugged myself, trying to ward off the pain that seared my heart. 'It's gone and I feel so…I feel so cold.'

The boy scowled and muttered, 'I didn't take your hat or your backpack. I wouldn't take nobody's backpack, ever. You ask me mates.'

'But you'd take the boots from my feet!' I cried.

He shrugged.

'What else did you take?'

'There wasn't nothin' else, was there? No stuff?' He was like a hungry farm dog sniffing meat.

'I don't know what you mean by "stuff". I had clothes and food.' Mum had put in enough dried foods for a week and now here I was with a ferl who had nothing.

'You're running out of food, aren't you?' I said, as if he were to blame.

'We got this bit here.' He pointed to a chunk of factory-made meat-bread and a finger-smeared bottle half filled with water. 'Want some?' he invited. This was a home of sorts. On a rickety shelf were some cups in a neat row, a yellow teapot and a metal bucket with a coiled rope attached.

'Thanks. I do need to eat. My head feels fuzzy again…I think I'm going to faint.'

'Have some water.' He put a cup to my lips 'You better like it, cos this is all we got.'

After I drank he broke the bread with his hands, counting the crumbs to make it fair. It had an odd fishy smell.

'Hold it in your mouth and chew,' he advised, 'then you won't chuck up.' I had to turn my face away from his filthy hands to stop myself wanting to chuck up right away.

'How long have you had this, a year?' I took a mouthful of the rank food, closing my eyes to chew. I have to keep it down, I thought. With food in my belly, I'll be able to think properly.

Before long, our meal was interrupted by a loud clatter on the roof.

'Who's that?' I whispered.

'Only me mate, Squibby,' said Shoeboy. 'He bangs like that so's I know who it is.'

A weedy-looking boy came in. Feet first. 'You there Shoeboy?' He nodded a kind of hello, shifting under my gaze. His eyes flicked to my boots and then Shoeboy. He grinned slyly. 'I heard about the orphan of Morwena.'

It took me a moment to realise he was talking about me. Orphan of Morwena? Is that what I am? Oh, my brother, little sister, I have to find you.

'Hey Squibby, have you eaten today?' Shoeboy looked at me expectantly. 'You give him a bit of your bread and I give him a bit of mine.'

'I wouldn't call it bread,' I muttered, but I broke off a third of what I had.

'Done any trading?' Shoeboy asked Squibby.

'Yeah, I been all the way to Camp B. You can trade but it's crowded with GRIMs so you got to watch your back.'

'Any food in them camps?' Shoeboy asked.

'I fronted and got told to bugger off.' Squibby went on chewing, hungrily. 'There's all these kids see, and they're getting 'em sorted. Even sending them to people like you-know-who, hah!'

He swigged some water from a flask in his pocket then offered it round but I couldn't bring myself to drink after him. I shook my head, trying to take in all that he said about the camps.

'Hey, Shoeboy, Alrica wants her.' Squibby threw me a look. 'Rattus took the orphan's backpack while yous was asleep. He gave it to Alrica and they talked about this one.'

Moodily, Shoeboy looked away. 'He had no bloody right to come in here. I don't want nothing to do with Rattus or Alrica.'

'Alrica will give you some first-grade stuff if you take the orphan there.' A flicker of cunning crossed his face. 'Hey you! Orphan of Morwena! Do you want them things of yours?'

'So, you know the thief who took my backpack?' I almost spat the words.

'Yeah,' Squibby muttered.

'It were Rattus,' Shoeboy said. 'He's Alrica's boy, but you don't get nothin' back from her unless you pay.'

'But that's not fair,' I cried.

'Fair don't come into it with Alrica,' said Shoeboy.

I tried to work out what the ferls were talking about. It was like a different language.

Squibby tapped Shoeboy on the shoulder. 'I see you're running out of food,' he said, slyly. 'You need some stuff to trade with, eh? I think you'd better take the orphan to the wolf woman.' He spat on his own hand and then held it out to Shoeboy.

'I don't know. I'm finished with Alrica,' said Shoeboy. 'Any rate, I'm getting a goat soon and when I do, I won't need Alrica nor nobody.'

'Aha,' the boy scoffed. 'You're always talking about getting a smelly old goat. How are you going to eat today?'

'I don't reckon the orphan ought to go there. Let Alrica have the bloody backpack,' Shoeboy grumbled.

Furious, I yelled at him, 'But that's not right. I'm going to get my backpack. I want my hat. My mum made me that hat.'

At this Shoeboy shrugged like a weary old man. He spat on his hand and slapped the other boy's palm, muttering a sullen, 'If this be a lie, slit me throat and leave me die.'

Squibby spat on his hand in the same way and held it out to me but I drew away from him. I wasn't a ferl and I didn't want any of their ferl ways.

8

House of Silver

We followed a trail through a plantation of trees overgrown with prickles and other natives. All the time I worried. I should find some adult to take care of things. What am I doing in this wild place with two boys who don't even have proper names?

Already weak with hunger, I licked cracked lips. Once or twice I stumbled. I had to stand still to stop myself from fainting. My mind played tricks on me. I tried to sort things out.

Why am I going to this woman? Is it for my hat or my backpack or both? And how is that connected to finding Bonnie and Andre?

I struggled on, complaining about my thirst. The salt from Shoeboy's meat-bread had made my tongue thick and dry. I stared at his back and hated him. He skipped along as though going without food and water were nothing. Even Squibby, who had seemed puny before, stood taller and straighter. By the time they stopped to rest I shook with anger.

'Don't you care…about anything?' I screamed. 'Don't you want food and water?'

Exhausted from my outburst, I sat on a fallen log with my head in my lap. Shoeboy sighed wearily. Calmly he went about plucking the spiky leaves of a grasstree and dividing the bunch in two, he handed me half. 'Chew the soft white ends,' he advised. 'Them's sweet.'

A warm rush of tears sprang to my eyes, 'Them's are,' I replied. Heaven help me, I sounded like a ferl.

We went on chewing the spike ends. Shoeboy grinned with one dirty hand held like a fan to his ear. 'Listen,' he commanded, 'and you'll hear what you want to hear. I thought it were close.'

At first, I heard nothing but the wind in the trees and the sound of parrots screeching. A crow let out a sad ka-ark. And then a sound came to me, flowing softly and secretively in the valley below. I jumped up and ran through the scrub. I didn't care about prickles tearing my legs and clothes. I pushed my way through sharp cutting reeds to the water, to a river – narrow, swift and deep.

I squatted on a rock. Making a cup of my hands, I scooped up water and drank my fill. I washed my bleeding legs. At once the stinging eased and I leaned over to wash my face. Dreamily, I took in the rich earthy colour of the river, the damp mossy smell of its bank.

I gazed into the water. A fallen leaf drifted and then sank to become part of the river bed's darkness. For a single moment I wanted to be that leaf with no thought and no fear, yet the river went on and it seemed to tell me 'so must you.'

Shoeboy touched my shoulder. 'We better go now.'

I came back to myself and with a surge of fresh energy, I strode through the bush, telling him, 'Just as soon as I get my hat, I'm going to find Bonnie. Then I'll find the others.'

'Who are the others?' he asked with shy curiosity.

'My brother, my cousins, and my friends, Jacob and Emily. When we find each other, we'll go home to our land.' As though words would make it all come true.

'Yeah?' said Shoeboy, brightening. 'And would there be room for a goat?'

'There'd be room for a goat.' I could see our land so clearly, but

I knew I must not allow myself to think of the sea. The sea was my enemy now.

Shoeboy led us away from the river to a pine plantation where the shadows closed in, where bright fungi grew like flowers on fallen logs. The build-up of pine needles muffled our footsteps, the silence broken only once when a flock of screeching cockatoos rose from the trees.

I counted, 'One for sorrow, two for joy, three for disappointment, four a letter, five a boy, six a girl….' A girl! It had to be Bonnie! Was this journey with the ferls bringing me any closer to her?

The untended part of the forest was overgrown and dark. In some places you couldn't see the sky. Some instinct told me it was the perfect opportunity to break away from the ferls altogether and begin my search for Bonnie. But I would be utterly alone. The moment passed and the thought of my hat drove me on.

Very soon my energy waned. 'How much further must we go?' I asked, wearily.

'A long way,' said Shoeboy.

'Without food?' My stomach clenched with hunger

He shrugged. 'You just got to do it.'

I picked up a fallen pine cone. Cockatoos ate the seeds, I remembered. But this was hard, like stone, the seeds hidden within tight interlocking cases. Taking a chance, I broke off a piece of fungi from a fallen log in passing. But rather than ease my hunger it messed with my head. I thought I was going home.

Soon I'll be there and I'll fall into Mum's arms. Dad will cook a special meal for me. Andre will sing his drummer girl song. But there's something to remember. Something I must do. Yes. There's an upside-down sky in the river and Bonnie has gone to deep water to find it.

'We're nearly there.' Shoeboy brought me back to myself and I staggered after him – down a steep slope and up a stony ridge. We stood together at the top, gawking at the scene below.

In a steep sided quarry, some fifty metres below us, there stood, not some shack or cave as I had expected, but a silver house with a shining solar roof and a garden of flowers and fruit trees of every kind. Relief flooded over me.

'That's where we go in.' Shoeboy waved to a spot further along the ridge. He said something but I hardly heard. I ran towards the silver house away from Shoeboy and all ferls, away from their roughly made shelters and their stale factory bread. Here was a real home, untouched by the Killer, with fruit and flowers and surely a kind grownup somebody who would help me find Bonnie.

But my legs wouldn't carry me. The world was falling on its head. Shoeboy's face was close to mine. I couldn't believe he was robbing me. His hand unclipped Mum's dilly-bag of seeds from my waist, but why? Why did you take them, Shoeboy?

9

An Angel

Somebody washed my body. They covered me with a quilt. It smelled clean, like lemons. 'You're safe here.' Soft fingers smoothed away my thick head. The woman fed me soup.

'You must be Alrica but you look like an angel.' Honey-coloured hair framed the woman's face. A kind face, surely. I so wanted it to be kind. Blue eyes crinkled into a smile. Of course, it was kind but why did my pulse leap when I looked past the blue of her eyes into the enormous pupils?

Struggle out of the bed with its stroking layers, I told myself. Tell the beautiful angel you can't possibly stay. But the pillows were like plump hands clutching me.

Words tumbled out of me, 'They said somebody called Rattus gave you my backpack. I need it because my hat is in the backpack and I must have my hat. My mum made it for me.'

'We have lots of hats here.' Alrica held a cup to my lips.

'You might have lots of hats, but they're not mine.'

'Hush now, Leila, drink the medicine. It will rest your troubled head.'

She didn't understand. My hat was gone and so were Mum's seeds. Now I had lost everything.

'Shoeboy took something from me,' I said. 'I want to see him so I can tell him off.'

'Shoeboy is a ferl. He's gone. You can't trust a ferl. But you are not to spoil things by worrying about what you have lost.'

Spoil things? Whatever did the woman mean? I wanted Mum's seeds. I wanted to take my hat and be gone.

I slept again, though I had no memory of sleeping, only of waking with the uncomfortable feeling that somebody watched my every move. Not once did she speak, though I called, 'Alrica?'

I saw her then. She stood in the room away from the small circle of light around the bed, as shadowy and dark as a bad dream.

'Why are you watching me? What do you want from me?' I grabbed the small solar lamp from the bedside table and thrust it forward so that I could see her more clearly. In the half-light, Alrica stood perfectly still. Her blue eyes, now dark and ravenous, never left my face.

Again, I asked, 'What do you want from me?' Slowly I put down the lamp and lay down, pulling the covers over my head. Like a small child, I rocked myself and whispered my sister's name, as if, by holding onto Bonnie, I could block out the shadowy thing that hung over me.

When next I woke, there were voices, Alrica saying, 'Show her the bathhouse, and then bring her to me.'

In a half stupor, it took me a moment to realise who had come into the room.

'Emily!'

'Don't say too much. Not here.' Emily had her finger on her lips. She helped me from the bed and then hurried me along a passage to a place of shining slate, of mirrors and flowing water. It bubbled into a heated pool from which Colly emerged, saying, 'So…it's you…'

Beside me Emily burst into tears. 'Hush…hush now, Emily,' I said, 'I'm glad you are both alive, but tell me, where's Jacob?'

'Oh Leila…Jacob is the only one of my family who was ever really there for me. And I don't know where he is.'

Slowly it came out. Emily and Colly had been in the city with Stefan. He knew an official and had managed to get them on an early train.

'Stefan wouldn't come with us,' Emily cried. 'He was trying to get places for other kids.'

'Colly?' My gaze rushed to hers but she turned away from me, her face a mask.

'I don't want to talk about Stefan. I don't want to think about Stefan. We are here now and we can't go back.'

Jacob…Stefan…both gone? What was left for any of us? Sick in my heart, sick in my gut, I struggled to stay standing. I retched and Colly threw me a towel.

'You're disgusting.' She turned away from the sight of me.

'Leave Leila be.' Emily flashed a look at Colly and then, when my nausea had eased, took the towel, washing it in a deep trough where water gushed and spilled in a cleansing stream.

'If only I had my clothes. That would be something.' Sitting on a stone bench, I felt naked and exposed in a flimsy nightdress.

'Alrica provides us with real clothes,' Colly said, 'not the home-spun things you wear.'

'But I want my homespun things. That woman is weird. I want to be out of here.' In miserable silence I looked at Emily. Her small face, usually lit with smiles, looked pinched and sad.

'Alrica is our foster-mother,' Emily said. 'She has signed papers. Now we are hers.' Then quickly, too quickly, 'She has been kind to us.'

'On the outside, people are starving,' Colly said. 'Here we have everything. Alrica chose us because she thought we were special.' A flush crept over her face. 'But she didn't choose you, so why are you here?'

'A ferl called Rattus took my backpack and gave it to Alrica, so

Shoeboy brought me here to get it back.'

'Hah! Shoeboy's nothing but a lying ferl.'

'No…no don't say that.' I was disappointed and angry with him for taking Mum's seeds. I felt betrayed by him, but I wanted to save him from Colly. I searched for words to defend him but she waved her arm at me.

'I'm not wasting my time talking about a ferl like him. Come now, Emily…and you too, now you are here. Alrica is waiting.'

A door at the end of a passage led to an airy room furnished with big soft chairs and bright cushions. The walls shimmered with painted flowers, animals and birds. A skylight flooded the room with morning sunlight.

'Welcome! Welcome, dear loves.' Now as soft and sheeny as a moth, Alrica offered us freshly baked bread and honey. As she moved between us, the silk of her long skirt brushed against our knees.

At first, I thought no, I won't eat her food, but I took a small piece of bread and an awful hunger took hold of me. I couldn't help stuffing my mouth with more. My hands shook as I picked up a teacup from the tray on offer and drank down the contents in noisy gulps.

Alrica's blue eyes crinkled into a smile. 'Be sure to drink it all.'

Maybe last night was a dream, I thought. Maybe she really does want to help me. I drained the bittersweet dregs of tea from the cup.

'You'll need some clothes, Leila.' She lifted the lid from a padded seat on which she had been sitting. I had never seen anything like it. Inside were dainty shoes, gold belts, shawls, hats and silk dresses in gorgeous colours.

'Now this one is surely yours, dear love.' Alrica held up a summer frock against me. It was blue-green, very much like my hat.

'Mrs…Alrica,' I blurted out. 'I came here to get my hat. Can I please have it? I really need to start looking for my baby sister.' I explained that I wanted to find my brother too. 'But at least Andre is old enough to take care of himself. Bonnie is only little and she's not used to strangers.'

'After you've rested we can talk about that. You do need to rest, don't you?'

I sat back in the cushions of a plump settee. It would be so easy to fall asleep this very moment, but I had to think of Bonnie. I had to have my things. I turned away from Alrica's face, away from the magnetic blue eyes.

'I want my backpack now,' I demanded. 'The ferl has used up my food, hasn't he? He's stolen my hat!'

'You're talking about Rattus,' Alrica said, calmly. 'He took care of your things so that Shoeboy wouldn't steal them.' She turned to Colly. 'Colly, do fetch Leila's things to put her mind at rest.'

When Colly handed me the backpack I was surprised and confused.

'Is there anything missing?' Alrica's triumphant eyes showed a glint of steal.

'Nothing is missing,' I stammered. 'I'm sorry for what I said and…thank you for the food and for helping me but I'm leaving now.'

'You must rest before you decide anything.' Alrica's voice came from far away. 'I've had one of my house-girls tidy your bed and instructed her to help you into it.' Her voice faded away. Again, I tasted the bitterness of her tea dregs and darkness closed over me.

This bed is so soft; I'm scared it might swallow me. I tried to call out but my tongue couldn't speak. My arms and legs wouldn't move, even when I felt the brush of a lemon-scented pillow across my face. For a few seconds it was there – I could have sworn it was there – against my nose and my mouth. I felt the power of strong arms behind it pressing harder and harder. I thought I would die and then suddenly it was released and Alrica hung over me.

'You will soon learn that your mother's hat is not for you, dear love.' Her whisper came like a bad odour wrapped in something sweet.

While I live, I'll never wear a hat of yours, I thought, never, ever.

10

A Creeping Mist

'Leila, wake up. Please, wake up.'

In the glow of the lamplight, my eyes focused on Emily's pale face while she explained how she had seen Alrica throw my things into the garbage, and how she had rescued them.

'I couldn't let her take away your hat without trying to get it.' Emily sat on the bed and let out a dry sob. 'When she threw your things out, her eyes were as mad as a rogue sheep dog turned killer. I'm scared of her, I'm scared of this place and the men who visit. I hate the way they look at me.'

At her words something in me hardened. My fear changed to anger and with it I felt my strength flooding back. 'Emily,' I said, 'I'm leaving and I think you should come too.'

'Yes, but somebody's coming. I'll be in terrible trouble if Alrica knows what I have done.'

A glimmer of light crept under the door and then Colly came in, wearing a long white nightgown. Her black hair fell round her shoulders like a shining curtain. It was held back by an amber comb that glowed richly against her darkness.

'What are you doing out of bed, Emily, and why are you blubbering?'

'Because she's frightened.' I climbed off the bed to stand level with Colly, eye to eye. 'There's something weird about this place, something bad. Alrica gave me some kind of drug to confuse me. She scared me half to death.'

'You're not dead,' Colly stated flatly. 'And you seem to be thinking for yourself. If Alrica scared you, you must have done something wrong.'

'Is it wrong to want my own things? Is it wrong to want to find Bonnie? I don't think so. I'm going away now and I've asked Emily to come too. Do you want to come with us?'

'Emily doesn't want to go with you. We're staying. You can go if you want. But I think you're mad.' Colly's cheeks flared with colour. Her dark eyes glittered with anger.

I turned to Emily. 'Emily, what do you want to do?'

'She's staying here.' Colly glared at me.

We waited in silence and then Emily said in a small tight voice, 'I'm going with Leila.'

'That's right! When it comes to it, you Hardies stick together. Oh, you're such a child, Emily, and as for you, Leila, I hate you. I hated you from the moment I saw you. Now get out of here...both of you. Go and starve if you want to.'

Colly's fury came like the sting of a wasp and I had to tell myself – it has nothing to do with me; it belongs to her. For Emily's sake and my own I couldn't let it crush me. I dressed in tough jungle green pants and my cape-jacket, trying not to show that I was trembling inside. I pulled on my boots.

'Leila, I don't have anything to wear because Alrica gives me the clothes she chooses for me each morning.' Beside me Emily shivered in thin pyjamas. On her feet she wore a dainty pair of red shoes with bows and tiny heels.

'I can give you long pants and a cape-jacket,' I told her, 'but the shoes will have to do.'

While I slipped into the harness of my backpack, Colly bundled up a quilt and pillow from the bed, tying it together with a scarf. 'If you're going to sleep in the dirt Emily, try and get hold of a ground sheet or bag,' she said, bossily. 'And now, Miss Clever One, how are you planning to get Emily and yourself out of here?' Colly went on to tell me about the locked doors in my way, and that if I'd planned to climb the hanging gardens that led to the lip of the quarry, I'd better think again. 'Those pretty plants are full of prickles, poisons and other nasties. Well?'

Before I could say a word, she took the comb from her hair and, with a twist of her fingers, produced a skeleton key from the comb's hollow centre. 'You're not the only one who has something precious.' Colly tossed her head proudly. 'My father made this for me. It's the only one of its kind and will take me anywhere.'

'If you hate me so much,' I said, 'how do I know you won't use it to lead me straight back to Alrica?'

'What kind of a person do you think I am? We're both children of Morwena, aren't we?' She motioned us to be quiet as she led us outside onto a porch.

'You're in luck. Alrica is away on business tonight. There's only Martin, the ground keeper, and soon he'll sneak into the kitchen to have tea with the house-girl. I'll get you out of here while he's there.'

Moist air from the wetlands nearby had caused the fog to enclose the garden like a thick blanket.

'I feel like I'm suffocating,' Emily whispered. That was the feeling it gave you. My own breath came, shallow and fast. I swallowed down my fear.

'Listen!' Colly warned.

The rattle of chains, a guard dog's snarl and then a man called out, 'Who's there?'

At once Colly spoke up. 'It's only me, Martin. Alrica's cat wanted to go out.'

'Bloody cat,' the man grumbled.

'You'll keep the dog chained for an hour?'

'What else can I do with the damn cat on the loose?'

'When I say go,' Colly whispered, 'we'll go through the security underpass. It leads to the main gate. You're on your own after that. Stay off the main path or you'll meet ferls. You'll have fifteen minutes or so before Martin does his rounds. That'll give me enough time to get back to the sitting room where the house-girl will find me asleep with a book on my lap.'

'Are you sure you won't come with us?' I asked.

'And live like a dirty ferl?' Our eyes met and held. She seemed younger than I in that moment, and not nearly as tough as she made out.

I tried again. 'Colly, believe me, Alrica is dangerous. Come with us. We'll get by. We'll find some others. And what about Stefan? He might have got out of Morwena and be looking for you.'

'Don't talk to me about Stefan. Do you think he's worrying about me? Of course not. He's too busy saving his precious bloody world, so why should I care about him? No, he can rot in a ferl's hole and starve for all I care.'

I tried to make her see. 'Stefan does care about the world. That's the way he is, but I know he cares about you, Colly. I've seen the way he looks at you.'

'Did care about me. Did. It's all gone. Now I'm here. Colly's whole body stiffened, but behind the anger and the pride I saw somebody who had put herself in danger for Emily and me.

'Alrica might…do something to hurt you if she knows you helped us.'

'You don't get it, do you? Alrica won't hurt me because she needs me more than I need her and besides, I'm smarter than she is.'

'Is smart enough for somebody so twisted?' I asked.

'Smart is always enough,' Colly said. We waited in silence until

47

a light flicked on in the kitchen window in the eastern wing of the house.

'Now!' Colly whispered, and we slipped into the garden following a path that led to the underpass. Here, Colly went to a security box and inserted her key. In a sudden panic, Emily rushed forward and slipped on the glassy floor even before the first door had closed behind us. Colly hissed a warning to be quiet while I grabbed Emily's arm to steady her. I skidded without falling but my boots clattered loudly, echoing in the hollow space. At the same time, the guard dog yowled.

'It's all right.' Emily touched my hand comfortingly, 'He always yowls when Martin leaves him.'

'Do shut up you two!' Colly marched ahead of us, leading us from one chamber into another, keeping us in line, telling us to hurry up and to watch our step, that we sounded like a couple of nanny goats with the noise we made.

In the second enclosure, I almost gagged from the build-up of stale air and then the solar torch Colly had been carrying flickered out. From there, we were forced to make our way in the dark with arms linked, our breathing laboured and heavy.

'This is it,' Colly said.

We stopped at once, sensing the solidity of another door in front of us. Colly made some kind of scanning movement with her key and silently the door opened. We breathed in sweet air and then hurried up the ramp flooded by moonlight.

Within moments Colly had us through the gate and we were on the outside. The night was unbelievably clear, so different from the swirling mist in the quarry below. I wanted to take off without waiting another second, but Emily whispered a warning, 'I can hear Rattus.'

'Hide in the hedgerow,' Colly hissed and Emily and I dived for cover under overhanging greenery. The ferl came steadily forward muttering a stream of foul words in singsong fashion. It was a weird kind of invocation.

As he came closer, I saw Colly exposed and vulnerable in bright moonlight as she wrestled with the heavy gate. I counted the slow passing of seconds. And then she was slamming the gate shut behind her with a juddering clang. The sound shocked the ferl into silence. By now he was so close I could hear his wheezy breath.

He stopped in puzzlement to peer through the gate.

'Alrica! Wolf woman!' he screamed, rattling the gate in rage. 'You cheated me. Your stuff was a dud. I got nothing for it but a beating. You owe me the girl. You owe me Leila Kieva.'

Beside me Emily drew in her breath but the small sound that escaped from her lips was silenced by my cupped hand over her mouth. At this, the ferl whipped around, peering into the hedgerow. A nightjar flapped out of the tree above us and then came Colly's scolding voice from somewhere quite near.

'Rattus! You should be gone from here. Ferls don't belong here after dark. Go! Go now or I'll have Martin sool the dog onto you!' The ferl spat out a filthy insult and then his footsteps could be heard, crackling over a litter of fallen leaves until he took up his strange lone chant.

'He's terrified of Martin's dog,' Emily sighed. I let her words go, but my mind leapt to the ferl who had screamed at me with hatred, I'll get you for this…girl! I shuddered, knowing that someday I would meet him face to face.

11

Women of the Forest

I didn't look back but when we came to the top of the hill Emily placed her hand on my arm. 'Leila, I couldn't do this by myself,' she said. 'You won't…ever go off without me?'

'Friends always look out for one another,' I told her, yet something stopped me from making the wholehearted promise she wanted to hear. We slipped into the pine forest, our footsteps muffled by the fallen pine needles.

'It's so quiet under the pines,' Emily murmured. 'When you don't make a sound, I feel like you've turned into air and that I'll turn into air, too.

'I'm here and I'm alive, Emily, and so are you. I know I'm alive because my breath is warm on my fingers and my shoulders hurt where my backpack digs in.'

'My lips are cold but my feet are burning,' she said. It became a kind of game, our words going back and forth, yet all the time I was listening for something else. When I heard the excited yelp of a dog I stopped.

'It could be Martin's dog chasing Rattus,' Emily whispered.

'Don't run. We'll tire too quickly if we run.' I shivered.

Emily cried out, 'What's the matter? When you're scared, it

freaks me out.'

'Sorry but I can't help thinking about the ferl.' He'd been in Shoeboy's cave while I slept. The very idea of him standing over me filled me with horror, yet somewhere in my brain, I knew he was like me, a person stumbling in the dark with no place to go.

'You said not to run,' Emily grumbled, 'So why did you run just then?'

'I didn't know I was running.' The dog's yelps and barking grew fainter and so we went on until we were numb with weariness and the moon had run its course. By then we had come out of the pine forest to a stand of gum trees and the sound of running water.

I gave it a name, 'Rivergum Flat.'

As we lay down on the ground, the night closed in and I felt Emily secretly cringing.

She whispered, 'I wish…I wish we had a lantern.'

'There's only the river and the trees here,' I said.

'And the sky,' Emily ventured. 'I can see the morning star.'

'Me too…let's make a wish.' Softly we sang a well-loved chant that had come down to us through the centuries.

Moon light, star bright, I see a star tonight. I wish I may, I wish I might, have the wish I wish tonight.

At last Emily's breathing evened out and I held my hat against my cheek. To soothe myself I imagined being at home in the garden planting things. The black soil of the flood plain came easily. But the sea…I must not allow myself to think of the sea. The sea is my enemy.

For three days we walked on, always within sight of the river. At night I slept lightly. The sigh of the wind, somewhere an animal stirring, even Emily's quiet breath – all were taken in and measured safe or unsafe, enemy or friend.

In the early hours of the fourth day I sat up, my heart beating hard in my chest. A young frightened voice called out, 'Are you children of Morwena?'

'Yes,' I called back.

A boy carrying a lantern approached, wanting to know if he and his two younger sisters could camp near us. They had been on Train C.

'The rescue people wanted us to go to a foster family but we're going to our uncle's farm. He wants us to live with him.'

By this time Emily was awake too. We were soon chatting to the family, even laughing, forgetting altogether that we were slowly running out of food, had no parents and were as homeless as a couple of ferls.

After the family moved on the next day, it hit me afresh. I had only enough mixed grain for one meal and a few cups of rice, but when I told Emily she didn't seem to take it in. She sat in the nest of her quilt, nursing her blistered feet, her uncombed hair shielding her eyes from me.

A few days before, we had cut at her red shoes with nail scissors, joking about her new "peep-toes" but now a mood of dark despair settled on us both.

Using water from the river, I made a mushy porridge from the mixed grain and together we ate from the pot in silence. Afterwards Emily dribbled salt water over her feet. I dressed them with ointment and then I took to the shoes again with scissors using bandages from my medical kit to keep them on her feet.

Slowing my pace to match Emily's, I led the way along a roo trail. Once we surprised a big boomer. He stood so tall and still he might have been a statue carved in wood. I gazed into his strange moon eyes and for seconds I saw a world safe and beautiful.

The silent bush snapped into life as he took off. Some metres away a doe with a joey in her pouch waited, with ears twitching. She raised her head and from far away there came the crack of a zap-gun. Emily edged closer.

'Somebody hunting,' I said.

Some hours later we rested on the riverbank and scooped up

earthy smelling water with our hands. Memories of Mum's spicy soups came to tease me but I pushed the daydreams out of my mind.

'We'll have some rice tonight.' I handed Emily some spikes from a grass-tree to chew on.

By mid-afternoon my shoulders ached and Emily's blistered feet were hurting. I did the "rest" sign with a palm to my cheek and Emily did the naming.

'Wattle Tree Grove.'

Yes. It felt right. But I was too tired to tell her so. Though it was day time, sleep came easily. Long and deep. Sweet and dreamless. I woke, knowing someone was near. Against the crimson sky a black figure swayed from side to side, and then dipped in a sweeping curtsy. 'What is it?' I shrieked, 'a giant raven?'

'It's not a raven!' Emily cried. 'It's a person!'

Dressed in a hooded black cape, a scrawny old woman leaned over us with a zap-gun in her hand.

'Are you going to kill us?' I cried. She was so close I could smell her smoky bush-tucker breath. 'Why are you bobbing up and down? What are you doing to us?'

She laughed, noisily, throwing back the hood of her cape. Beneath her cape she wore some old rag and a shiny metal disk that hung from her scrawny neck. As it swung back and forth we followed it with our eyes.

'LIV,' I spelled out the letters inscribed on the disk.

'Who are you?' I demanded and what's that shining thing around your neck? Did you steal it?'

The woman scowled. 'I earned this medal and I earned it well. What about you…but let me guess, you are orphans of Morwena and you have run away from Alrica, the wolf woman!'

Emily screamed while I drew in my breath, frightened and angry. 'We ran away from her and we're not going back. You can't make us!'

The old woman's body shook with laughter. 'No, but the kops can if Alrica is your foster mother and they have a mind to.' She gave Emily a wink and a nod. 'But don't worry, they know better than to ask an old Hardie any leading questions.'

She was a Hardie, she told us, one of a few elders with a licence to shoot. Her face was as dried out as an old leaf but I saw nothing to fear in it. I told her about looking for Bonnie. 'I'm going to try the emergency camps for news. Every one of them if I have to.'

'If she's in one of them camps, get her out as fast as you can,' she advised. 'They give the poor mites watery soup. It makes 'em so weak they can't hardly squash a grape, even if they had one and they get skin ruptures because they don't get no greens.' The old lady scratched at her wiry hair. 'All the best food gets taken by the people from GRIM. But if you know what's sweet and safe to eat, you can't beat the old bush tucker.'

I tried to listen politely but my eyes popped when I saw a head louse peeping out of the grey strands of her hair. She told us her daughter was the Moccasin Maker. 'She keeps a shop along there a bit – makes slippers and grows a bit of spinach and so on.'

Her sharp eyes searched my face. 'Haven't seen a big roo buck, have you? I been chasing the devil for days.'

I glanced at Emily with a slight shake of my head.

'Not that I remember.'

'Not specially.'

'Too bad…but if you follow the wattle grove, you'll come to the shop.' The old woman reached far into her baggy cape. She pulled out a sprig of leaves. 'Give her these and she'll know you've seen me. She'll give you food and a roof for the night.'

After she had gone we argued about what to do.

'I didn't like the look of that old woman,' Emily wasn't happy. 'But she didn't hurt us, did she?'

'I still don't trust her and I wouldn't trust any daughter of hers.'

'Then we'll need to get off the track and camp in the bush for the night.'

'No! I don't want to spend another night in the bush. Oh, my feet are hurting! What are we going to do?'

'Emily, we need a proper rest. We need some good hot food. I can see a light up ahead. If it's the shop I think we should take a look. If we don't like it, we don't have to stay.'

The place was rubble but a shack had been fixed beside it and a sign said: Moccasins made to measure in exchange for animo fat, oil, honey or hard cash. See palmist-psychic for fortune-telling.

The old lady's message of leaves was thrown into a big pot of simmering food which gave off a delicious tang of spices and meat.

'You can call me Bess.' Flinty eyed and sharp in her ways, the shop keeper took the rice I gave her with a curt nod. While she cooked at an open fire, she juggled a baby boy who snuffled at her breast.

Emily looked at me and we nodded. We would stay. By candle light we ate the rich stew of meat and vegetables with fluffy white rice. As much as we wanted. After the meal we sat at the table and watched how the woman made the moccasins from skins – rabbit, possum, fox and roo.

I ran my hand over the lovely pelt of a roo and I saw Bess eyeing me. 'My old mother brings me the skins for my business and I do well.' She picked up a handful of paper money from a box and with a disgusted shrug, threw it back again. 'Forget this. It's hard coinage and things people use that gets you by these days.'

She went on about the news she heard from passing travellers. Our country had been taken over by the Union of All Nations. And did we know that Vesrigo had used its own weapon to wipe out Norland's heart? Now they were at each other's throats and poor as mice.

'The people who die are people like you and me. Nobody wins in the end except GRIM. Those bast'ds feed when the world turns into a garbage pit. They feed on kids like you. Oh, it makes me wild.'

When the candle burned low, Bess put down her needle and gave us herbal tea in small clay pots.

'I read palms for free when I'm good and ready and in the mood,' she told us between sips of tea.

'Will you read ours?' Eagerly Emily put out her hand. 'Please…read ours.'

I didn't believe a word of it but I wanted to hear what she had to say. Bess peered into Emily's hand, steadying it with her own. 'There's going to be three promises of wedded bliss in your life…maybe four.'

'And children?'

'You'll have four, I think. Two sets of twins…hmm…you'll live a long life…almost forever…and you'll never be alone…not like some I know.'

'What about me?' I held out my hand, disappointed when the woman seemed fidgety. 'Please?' It suddenly seemed important that she take it. As if my very life depended upon it.

Unwillingly she ran a scratchy finger over my palm. 'There's one true love here…and another who loves you. Mind that one doesn't break your heart.' She shook her head. 'Ah but you'll know what being alone means.'

I was angry. 'That's no kind of fortune. You haven't told me anything. Will I find Bonnie?'

'Now you've messed with my concentration.' She pushed my hand away and spoke sharply. 'It's time you two were in bed.'

We all slept on the earth floor with the fire flickering. The child woke in the night, cooing softly and his mother lifted him to her breast. A memory of Bonnie came to me – her soft little hands opening to touch the light – the smell of her hair. I turned my face to the wall. Bonnie…Bonnie…where are you, Bihbi?

12

Bonnie
A Child Without a Name

Little sister, you had your feather quilt to keep you warm, but no voice, not even the words that said your name. The gold name bracelet Mum and Dad gave you at birth had been taken from you. A silent thief in the night.

Bonnie didn't know she was in a refuge for young children. All night long oil lanterns flickered. Yellow…orange…blue. Monster shadows of the rescue workers leapt to yah and yaw at her from the canvas walls.

One day I would learn this from the woman who had worked in the refuge and from Tyke, a boy we called the Insect Collector. He was half-brother to Zara, the drummer girl who had lived with her father in our village.

When the rescue workers came near her bed Bonnie lay as still as a white bird that lives on the marshes of the Tanjin River. As though she guessed such stillness would stop strangers from bothering her about having no name. She would sigh when they moved onto the children who cried out in their sleep.

The rescue workers wondered about the little girl who had no voice. Her age could only be guessed at. Around three, they thought.

'Is there nothing at all?' the chief medic asked, 'Nothing to tell us who she might be?'

'Only the clothes she had on and a quilt. She won't let it out of her sight.' A happy feather quilt: green grass, yellow ducks, blue sky.

'I don't suppose anyone will claim her. It's been too long. A name, if only we had a name...hey little girl what's your name?'

Tiredly the medic moved on muttering about the child's chances of survival in such a place as this –Westland – brought to its knees with only a handful of UAN people to guide it.

'If only that child could speak,' the woman said.

She didn't know the words that surely played inside your head. In clusters, like beads on a string. Words spoken by Mum, the coach driver and passengers that marked the end of everything you knew.

One day Tyke would tell me how he was squeezed into a coach by his mother who paid in gold for his place.

There is no standing room in the coach, even for a child but a woman stands in its path, challenging the driver to stop or run her down. 'Please take my little girl to safety.'

'The coach is full, lady; I'll take not a single person more.'

The people shout, 'Take the child...we'll make room...take her.' Until at last, he agrees and everyone is silent. In the glare of the headlights Tyke sees the woman fasten a bracelet around her little girl's wrist. He hears her say, 'This is your name. This is your feather quilt. Your sister and brother will find you.'

A last moment with Mum, the warm musky scent of her and then she is gone. Bonnie is handed over heads from one person to another. 'Hush, little one.' A woman holds you. A kind woman but she has the powdery scent of a stranger. Her lap is not Mum's lap. An angry man says, 'Let the child cry for pity's sake.'

In the refuge, Bonnie didn't want the medic with his sharp needle. It jabbed her arm. Blood oozed onto her quilt. 'That must have hurt,' he mutters, 'You'd expect her to cry.'

He didn't know about the silent tears you wept. When it was Tyke's turn for a jab he yelled and bawled. He kicked the medic's shin. Angry words.

'Ouch, you little monster!'

Bonnie's face burned with fever. Her arm swelled. She drifted in and out of sleep. A lady fed her soup. A man gave her yellow vita-pills. Days and nights flickered like shadows.

If only she could speak, Mum would tell you. 'Don't be afraid, Leila and Andre will find you.'

It was Tyke the Insect Collector who brought you back with his big shiny eyes and a small pointy face. He chirped like a cricket and you wanted to be a chirping cricket too.

'You spoke!' Tyke cried.

When the lady came with soup Bonnie ate hungrily. To Tyke, she called herself Bihbi, but nobody else ever heard her speak. Every day she would peer into the faces of strangers, people who came for their lost children. But for her there was nobody.

Tyke shouted and cried, 'I want to go out and find Zara. She's a drummer. If I hear her, I'll find her. Let me out!'

The woman explained that the towns and cities of Westland were in ruin. It was a dangerous place for young children.

'I'm not young, I'm eight,' Tyke bawled. 'And I can feed myself from bush tucker. I live with my mum and she shows me how.'

The woman had to be stern. 'There's no place for young children out there.'

Every day the woman saw Bonnie and Tyke standing near the wire mesh fence that enclosed the refuge, waiting and waiting. Soon, soon your sister and brother will find you...soon...soon. That's what Mum had said.

13

The Moccasin Maker

While Emily chuckled over the baby, I couldn't even look at him without thinking, if only it were Bonnie. My empty arms ached for her. At night I went to sleep muddled from trying to work out how many more hours I would need to work so that I could be off again to look for her.

I had expected to leave the Moccasins Maker within two days but as she pointed out, the nearest camp was up to four weeks away by foot with a wasteland in between.

'I think you should stay here until Emily's feet are better. You can each work half a day for your keep and the other half for the dried food you'll need for your travels.' Emily picked up a needle at once and in no time at all she made a pair of slippers which the women examined without speaking. She gave a satisfied nod and then turned to the slipper I had laboured over.

'Bootlace stitches,' she cried in disgust, 'You can weed the garden, missy.'

I was set to work on a patch of gravelly soil – so different from the rich black soil I knew. I pulled at some deep-rooted couch grass between spinach plants, all the while fretting over lost time. To keep the plants alive, I had to lug buckets of water from a foul-smelling soak. The hours fell into one another drearily. I almost forgot what it was that I longed for.

Meanwhile, one of the blisters on the back of Emily's right foot turned into a running sore and then something else above her ankle. When Bess swabbed the sores with her crude antiseptic, Emily whimpered, 'My brother's ointments never sting like this…. Oh, Jacob, I wish you were here.' Clinging to my hand she bit on the corner of her quilt to stop herself from crying out. Only when the pain had eased did the tears slide along her cheek. Then she would tell me what a good friend I was to be there for her.

At this I had to stop myself from crying too, for I would remember the night that had just passed when I wanted to take what little food I had and be gone, with or without Emily. I so wanted to begin my search for Bonnie.

Feeling trapped, I began to see the woman in a different way, suspecting her of some kind of mischief. Whenever I could I peered into her jars and pots in which she mixed her 'cures' wondering if they contained some kind of poison. I longed for Jacob with his gentle wisdom. He'd know at once if anything was wrong and he'd know what I should do for Emily's feet.

My lack of trust in Bess became a poison in itself. 'What are those red streaks on Emily's legs? And why is she so hot?' I demanded, my voice rising with anger.

My cheeks burned when she snapped at me, 'I'm not a magician.' Then she calmed down a little to say, 'You're right, Emily shouldn't be this sick.'

I mumbled a 'sorry' and she went on to tell me the worst of the infections had turned into a two headed boil.

'It'll have to be cleaned up but it isn't ripe yet. I'll get her fever down, then try a honey cure and feed her more greens, strawberries and tea. So, Missy, while I see to Emily, you weed the spinach and strawberry patch and keep them well watered.'

That night, while Emily tossed and turned on her swag, Bess

passed a needle through the flame of a candle and then nodded to me. 'Hold the lantern close and be ready with a cloth. I'm going to clean this thing up.'

Kneeling beside Emily, she pricked the skin and with the heels of her hands, one on either side of the bluish-red swelling, she pressed down hard. Through gritted teeth, she snarled, 'We need the cloth now,' and Emily's muffled whimpers rose to a scream.

I watched with terrible fascination the build-up of matter bursting through the stretched skin at the carbuncle head. It shot into the cloth with a force that shocked me.

'Now take a clean cloth and hold it closer.' Bess ordered.

By now Emily was almost fainting. A sob stuck in my own throat at the sight of her white face but I could do nothing but sniff away my tears.

'Didn't I say to keep the lamp still?' Bess cried, harshly, but she flashed me a look that kept my hand steady and murmured. 'If I don't get everything out, this girl will die of blood poisoning.'

A few minutes rest and Bess began again, slowly building up the pressure until two solid cores of matter were lifted from Emily's bruised flesh. A single scream from Emily and then a clean flow of bright blood sprung from the wound. It was over. That night Emily slept without stirring.

A morning came soon after when the Moccasin Maker took me aside. By now Emily was the proud owner of new pants and cape and a strong pair of moccasins, all made by her own hands. Her feet were healed and I had a supply of grain, dried vegetables, biltong and tea, even a pot of honey.

'I've been told by a customer about a child in Camp B,' Bess said. 'A little girl with no name – she could be your Bonnie.'

'It has to be Bonnie!' My face turned scarlet. I wanted to laugh and cry at the same time. I picked up her baby, playfully threw him in the air and caught him. Soon, very soon, I'll have Bonnie in my arms, I thought. He chuckled and I laughed aloud. 'Goodbye baby,'

I sang. Making solar-plane noises, I held him above me as I raced inside to tell Emily.

'You needn't say a word. I heard it all.' Sitting cross-legged on her swag, she went on stitching the moccasin in her hand.

'You heard what Bess said. Great news, isn't it?' I rushed on, my words tripping over each other. 'Once we find Bonnie, we'll look for Jacob and Andre.'

'What if our brothers are dead?' Emily said, 'It would all be for nothing.'

'What…what are you saying?'

'I'm saying how dark and rough it is out there. What if ferls steal our food? Do we starve? What if the kops find me and take me back to Alrica? What if my feet get sore and my blood goes bad? I couldn't go through that again. I would die. I won't go. You can't make me go.'

'I would never make you do anything, Emily,' I said, 'you can stay with Bess if you want to.'

She turned to me with stricken eyes. 'But I don't want to be here with just Bess and the baby. Can't you stay? Won't Bonnie be all right in the camp?'

The baby, straddled on my hip, looked on with large solemn eyes. 'How can you say that? Bonnie isn't much older than him. You heard what the old hunter said about the camps. Don't make me feel bad for wanting to go to her.'

I held back tears of disappointment and anger, trying not to think of the days I had lost, but now Emily's shoulders shook and she sobbed, 'Oh I know you are right but I can't help feeling what I feel.' She cried some more and then went on. 'I'm afraid I'll never see you again, that if that child isn't Bonnie, you'll keep going to the next camp and the next.'

The baby squirmed out of my arms and ran outside to his mother while I sat down beside Emily, saying nothing, because what she said was true. I would go on until I found Bonnie. I could do nothing but hold her and tell her, 'We'll come through this, Emily, somehow we'll come through this.'

In the morning Bess gave me a plaited leather necklace, with a red heart at the centre where the letters LIV had been worked with fine stitches in gold thread. 'You've earned this I reckon, so wear it under your vest and be careful who sees it.'

I remembered the old Hardie, with her shining disk with that same word inscribed across its surface: LIV. 'Earned it? How have I earned it? I haven't done anything.'

'If you haven't already, then you will,' she said.

'But what does it mean?' I asked.

'You'll find out in time.' The woman's flinty face told me nothing but her voice softened. 'This is no palace, but Emily will eat well here and the handcrafts I can teach her will give her a living.'

Bess warned me about the wasteland ahead.

'When you get to the old minefields, only camp under Sheoak or where green reeds grow and look for something living in water before you trust it.'

When the time came for parting Emily gave me a pretty anklet to wear above my left boot and I gave her a bottle of the oil we used to keep little critters out of our hair. Just the thought of it had us both scratching our heads and although close to tears we broke into a fit of giggles. 'We haven't got em yet,' I said, 'but when the old hunter comes by, watch out.'

14

A Shattered City

I left the safety of a land I knew for a land of false promises, where shining lakes and gleaming cities beckoned, and then dissolved or shifted – always just out of reach. Maddening. But I would tell myself, every step I take is a step nearer to finding Bonnie.

Salt-encrusted mudflats gave way to a mountain range that had been scoured and picked over by generations of miners. The moon-like surface was marked by deep pits filled with a toxic green sludge or I might be surprised by an expanse of bright blue water surrounded by slagheaps where a she-oak grew. I would camp under its shelter listening to the sighing wind in its needles.

I came one day to a lake rimmed with green reeds which served as a breeding place for tiny colourless fish. Their lack of colour and sick mutations made me uneasy but I swam in there, diving into the water until a sense of the lake's depth and strange silence sent me scurrying out of the water and away. I was lonely for a human voice.

Within days I moved onto a valley where wild grasses grew. The air here was moist and cool, alive with the friendly sound of cattle lowing and the chug-chug of a machine. A hydro-fuelled truck trundled past me and then an animo cart loaded with grain. Two girls on a wind-charged sail bike waved at me as they passed. Later I would see them tangled in a ditch cursing the trader who sold them a dud.

As I lent them a hand, they asked, 'Are you an orphan of Morwena?' In the days ahead, I met others who would ask the same question. Kids like me looking for a brother or a sister or just someplace to go. 'Do you want to stick with us?' they might ask and I would say, 'I can't stick with anyone yet…not until I find my little sister and my brother.'

One night a family shared hot food with me in exchange for some dried spinach and carrots.

'We scoop up grain that falls from the trading carts,' the older sister, told me. She made wheatmeal porridge and then baked the left-over wheat on hot stones to be used like coffee grains for hot drinks.

When her brother came to the fire with a couple of rabbits he had snared, I wrinkled up my nose at the stink of death. The small bodies hadn't yet grown cold, but I watched to learn – the way he snipped at the inner legs and rolled the skin towards the head.

In time I would become an expert myself and if anyone gave me so much as a sideways look I would snap at them, 'We have to live, don't we?'

I always left at daybreak, before anyone else stirred. I pushed myself hard. A child with no name. Bonnie. It has to be Bonnie.

I expected to find Camp B standing like some kind of beacon, but instead, I found a shattered city, the survivors swarming like ants. There was a rumour that a fleet of supply trucks were coming with food.

'Can you tell me where to find Camp B…it's a refuge for young children.' I tried to make myself heard above the din – people pushing for a place in the queues zigzagging between the ruins.

'You need your hand stamped before you get anything,' a boy

warned me. The stamping had been done the day before – to stop profiteering, he told me. Later I heard a woman screaming, 'Tell that to my hungry kids. We've walked half the night to get here today.'

The boy didn't know there was a refuge for young children. He told me if I wanted to 'pinch' food it was easy enough to do it in the market place after the supply truck had been.

At that moment a cry went up, 'Here they are…here they are,' and the road trains rolled in, great snorting monsters hissing steam. Behind the trains there came a fleet of zip-cars, one with a trailer behind it, blazing a Voice of World sign. Young Soldiers of Peace set up solar powered info machines. They were there to register names and to hear what people had to tell.

But the voices I heard were like the roar of a wave.

'I want to know where to find Camp B, the refuge for young children.' I hadn't a hope of being heard. After what felt like hours, the food truck was still surrounded by milling people but there was a lull around the Voice of World team. A great hulk of a man must have been watching me because he whispered in my ear. 'Nobody will hear you unless you're seen.' He offered me his hand as a foothold and heaved me onto the Voice of World trailer.

'I'm looking for my little sister,' I yelled. 'I'm Leila Kieva. Can anyone take me to Camp B, the refuge for young children?'

A security kop called out, 'You are trespassing, girl.' So, I dropped to the ground and hid among the crowd. I hurried on, wanting to leave the kop well behind when I heard a voice, 'Leila Kieva!'

A young Soldier of Peace leapt from a moving zip-car and ran towards me. He'd grown gaunt and thin, but his eyes gleamed. Laughing eyes. For a moment I thought he was going to kiss me.

'Stefan!' I couldn't drag my eyes from his face.

The driver of the zip-car called out, 'I said two minutes, Stefan. No more!' Stefan waved to the driver and smiled at me. He went on smiling. 'I heard you…I heard your name. Are you travelling by yourself?'

I nodded, unable to speak, as if all my words had dried up. And then he said, 'I'm going south. I'll be in trouble if I don't go now, but why don't you come with me?'

The light in his eyes and the warmth of his hand on mine was something I could never quite forget no matter how hard I tried, but I shook my head. 'Why…why should I go with you?'

'I don't know. I just think it would be good for us both. You could be one of us. We work all over the world. Right now, we're helping kids who've been caught up with GRIM.'

'Then help Colly,' I blurted before I could stop myself. 'She's with Alrica, the wolf woman.'

The driver beeped again. A voice from the passing crowd called out, 'Go home Norlander basted. You can't make up for what your Top Controller did to us.'

'Yes…I'm a Norlander,' Stefan shouted back, 'but I'm a citizen of the world first.' And then to me, 'Leila…I'll do what I can for Colly, but I still want you to come with me.'

I shook my head again.

'Come on,' the driver called out once more. Stefan leapt onto the back seat of the open zip-car, calling out as the car moved on, 'Leila, if ever you change your mind send a message through the LIV people. One day we'll be together.'

No Stefan, I thought. I have Bonnie to find and I have to make a garden for her. I watched until he was out of sight, wondering about how far the zip-car would take him in a day, wondering about Stefan and the path I might have taken if I'd gone with him. I didn't know then, that one day his name would be written into Westland's history as a pioneer in opening free info-centres for our people.

In the market place I sheltered from the heat of the sun in a burnt-out house wondering what to do next, when an old woman with twinkling eyes appeared where a window should have been. 'Oh, my dear,' she said in her soft, rapid way, 'I've been chasing you since you stood on the trailer.'

She reminded me that I had fingered my necklace as I spoke out. It made her think I might have come from the Moccasin Maker. She pulled something from her own wizened chest. It was a LIV sign like the one Bess had given me. 'We don't break the law,' she murmured. 'But we know how to bend it to help young people like you. I can bribe someone to let you into the refuge if you like.'

A wisp of a woman, but nimble and quick as somebody quite young, she wrote my name and the date on a message board and then led me through the ruins. My spirits lifted as I scrambled after her. In this part of the city a line of family huts had been built, complete with solar panels and garden plots. From somewhere a woman called out in a reedy voice, 'Get your fortune told for hard cash or goat's milk.'

It was life going on, like a river finding its way after a flood. I too will learn to trade, I thought. I'll make a shelter for Bonnie and I'll hire myself out, working in somebody's garden for food and some seeds. For a moment I sensed Mum's presence so strongly I could almost feel the brush of her long hair against my arm and the warmth of her body near me.

I told her: Oh Mum, I'm sorry I lost your seeds, but I'm almost certain to find Bonnie in this refuge. And then I'll start my own collection of seeds for our land.

Grey and low, the refuge was more like a prison than a place for young children. I wanted to find Bonnie and snatch her away.

'It is against regulations to hand over a child to somebody so young,' the manager told me, 'or to take bribes.' He looked hard at the LIV woman, who looked away, and then went on, 'but there's a sickness of heart in these children that no medic will ever fix so if your sister is here, then take her. As you can see there is more than one child whose birth name has been lost.'

The little ones followed me with their eyes.

'None of these are Bonnie,' I whispered.

The man sighed. 'Then I have nothing for you…except…there is a child in the sick-bay. She is suffering from a resistant viral sickness.'

'It has to be Bonnie,' I said.

The child was crying softly as if she didn't even hope that anyone might hear.

'She could be infectious,' the man warned, but I was already leaning over a little girl with golden hair and sad blue eyes. I shook my head.

The LIV woman touched my hand. 'I'll be camped near the wall where I wrote your name.'

I thanked her and then trudged heavily along a path that led to the bush reserve above the town. Tired beyond measure, I curled up on the bare ground, indifferent to what might happen to me. I had drifted into a half dream when a group of little kids from a settlement came by to poke at me.

'Is she dead or alive?'

'Awake or asleep?'

Holding my hat close to my cheek, I stared into round upside-down eyes and rosy mouths. Like butterflies, I thought, but those butterflies had stings. They took my backpack and flew to their butterfly homes.

'Oh Andre, I need you brother.' I cried inside for Bonnie, for the blue-eyed nameless baby of the refuge and for myself.

15

Andre: Singer

While I cried for him, Andre dreamed of the Killer. Always the same dream. An implosion like an indrawn breath. The deep rumble of the earth beneath him. For nights on end he would relive the scene. The so called 'refuge' disintegrating around him. Kop sirens wail. A sensation of falling. Down – into a strange, still pool. Blood red, jagged, blinded, he is the fish on a barbed hook.

There are voices: Huldah, Tristan, and Zara.

'Run, and don't stop running. There could be fires and gas leaks.'

'But what about Andre?'

Huldah says, 'It's too dangerous to go back into that building. Don't stand there gaping. Help me. Zara's in shock. Let's get her to safety.'

Andre never let go of his guitar. Hours might have passed, or days until he found an inner wall. But the wall turned into a tunnel made of oil trees on our land. Mum and Dad were there with liquid limbs and dream voices.

Mum tells him there are still songs to write and a life to live but it is Dad who urges him to fill his lungs where the fresh air blows in and to sing so that somebody will hear him. More time passes and then, in the dark wreckage, a hand reaches out to touch him. There are Voices.

'There's somebody alive…a boy.'

'He'll lose the sight of that left eye.'

'He'll be scarred.'

'We heard him singing in the ruin.'

They called him 'Singer'.

Andre measured time in terms of pain and no-pain, until one morning he touched the bed cover where sunlight fell. He raised his arm and saw blue veins, his blood doing its work. I've come through it, he thought. I'm alive.

Huldah and Tristan came to the surgeon's clinic to see him. 'Our dad, our gran and your parents never got out. There are only we three, now.' Huldah had seen a man who was supposed to know.

'Yes.' Andre didn't need to be told.

'But Leila and Bonnie will be somewhere,' said Tristan. Ever hopeful he went on about a man called Rick who would fix everything. 'He's finding out about our families and he's helping us find a home.'

'What about Zara? Andre asked, uneasily.

'We are taking care of her,' Huldah said, 'but there's something wrong.'

As if the life had been squeezed out of her. When she came to see him, she sat on Andre's blind side.

'I guess I make a pretty sight.' Andre made some silly joke about Camp A. 'It used to be a kid's holiday camp…some holiday we had.'

'There's nothing left for us,' Zara said.

Andre wanted to tell her, 'We still have each other.' But she went on talking in circles about her parents and her little brother, Tyke. The man called Rick had told her Tyke was dead.

'He lived with our mum…I was supposed to visit last weekend

and I missed it. Andre, he was eight years old.'

Andre could only say, 'Sorry.' How weak and useless it seemed. For days afterwards, he thought of things he might say to her. He would tell her about being caught in the ruin, about his mum and dad being with him. He would tell her about the miracle of being found. Surely that wasn't for nothing.

When Zara came, the carefully thought out words died on his lips. There was a difference in her. A warm inner glow, like somebody who'd found a new religion.

'I'm going with Rick. He's helped me come alive again. He's going to let us work for our living. We'll be paid. He's giving us a home. Tristan and Huldah are coming with me.'

Tears stung Andre's unhealed wounds. He pictured the surgeon's stitches under the white gauze shrouding his face, like rows of tiny crosses on a purple-tinted scar. You're alone and you're not pretty any more, but you are alive, aren't you? He rode the pain like a surfer rides a wave. Find the cool green hollow; let it go, let it go.

When it was time for Andre to leave, the clinic manager told him an anonymous mentor had paid his debt to the surgeon. The woman showed him the account and the money received. It was more buks that Andre had ever seen.

'It's the only way we can keep the clinic going.'

So, I'm in debt to a stranger. Andre owned nothing but his guitar, and after hours standing at the end of a queue, some food rations and a swag.

'We're finding places for younger children,' the UAN worker told him, but you older ones are on your own.' He drew a map in the sand, pointing out the position of a roadside tavern. 'You'll be given another lot of rations. You might pick up paid farm work with somebody who recruits workers from there.'

On his journey south, Andre passed villages where nobody had survived the ripple effect of the Killer. He'd never known such silence. Nothing but the buzz of insects. Sometimes the call of a bird. At sunset his shadow took on a life of its own. A hump of swag. A peaked hat. An outline of guitar. Like some fairy-tale creature come to life. A singer without a song.

The nights were clear. He tried to make a song but there was nothing in him. He lay down on his swag, looking at the sky, looking at the universe. Time stretched on forever didn't it? Yet Mum's life and Dad's life flashed only once.

After two days without food, Andre knew he was in trouble. The solid world he knew became illusory, full of shadows and uncertainty. Sometimes he thought he was among night-scroungers and ferls who had to beg or rob in order to live.

'Must I live like you?' he shouted to grey ghosts as he passed through a village where there were no survivors to bury the dead. He pushed on, fearing nightmares that would surely come with sleep.

At last he welcomed the solidity of a tavern with a warm light glowing in the window. A large framed woman let him in but regarded him sourly.

'So, you're another orphan of Morwena who thinks he'll get rations here. My food comes from these!' She thrust her hands towards his face. 'If you eat here, you pay.'

Andre could do nothing but show her his empty purse. He had used the money his dad gave him to get out of Morwena. He gazed at her blankly.

'Ah but you have your guitar.' The woman squinted at him shrewdly. 'If you trade it, I'll give you a feed and a bed for the night.'

It was as if she'd asked for his seeing eye.

'Don't take the boy's guitar!' A man with brilliant blue eyes and a thick thatch of hair came forward, putting out his hand. 'I'm Rick and you must be Andre. One of my UAN friends told me about you. You're the one they call Singer.'

Just to hear his name spoken warmed him. It was Andre's first human contact in days.

'Tristan and Huldah are your cousins and Zara, a friend. Is that right? They asked me to look out for you.'

'Zara asked you to look out for me?'

'Yes…yes…I'm sure she'll be pleased to see you.' Rick signalled the innkeeper. 'Give the boy a meal, Candy. I reckon the farm will pay. We could use a singer down there, isn't that right Snow?'

'Yeah, I reckon we could.' The man's curious gaze drifted to Andre and then slid away. It reminded Andre of what a scarecrow he must look, how scarred and hollow. But now Candy was setting out a rich brew of soup. Food he knew he was going to accept. He fumbled for a spoon and it clattered onto the floor.

For a moment there was silence, and then Rick was saying in an easy way, 'It must be hellish trying to get used to a blind eye. Candy, how about another spoon for the Singer?'

Somehow it made him feel whole again, not just a scarred kid with an empty belly. He understood now why Zara had been so taken with Rick. He knows, Andre thought, he really knows how it is for me.

Rick ordered food for himself, 'to keep the boy company,' he said, and they tucked in without speaking, sharing a freshly baked loaf of bread. Gradually Andre felt the soup warming him. His chilled hands and feet tingled back to life. His head cleared.

If Andre signed on with the farm he'd earn his keep and be paid in cash at the end. 'Snow is the foreman and he'll keep a tally on how much we owe you.' Rick had even thought of family and when Andre told him what little he knew, he promised to sort it out. 'We get to know what goes on in the camps and we'll find out about your sisters.'

Andre slept that night without nightmares or flashbacks. Drifting off to sleep he wondered what they grew on the farm. He pictured fields of canola, ripening corn and sunflowers with great yellow faces. A fuzzy dream of a future came to him. Rick will help me find Leila and Bonnie. When the city is safe, we'll go back to Morwena. We'll work our land. We'll make a home.

In the morning Andre saw Rick put some boxes into a hydro-fuelled truck marked with a friendly Union of All Nations sign, the distinctive UAN. A surge of energy flowed through his veins. Rick works with the backing of the Union of All Nations, he thought. He grows food for people of this land who are suffering so much hardship. That's why he has precious fuel cells and supplies.

A small moment of doubt. 'Why…why is the driver wearing a zap-gun?' Zap-guns could only be used by a few elders if they had a special licence for hunting or to kill a dying animal. That had been the law for as long as Andre could remember.

Rick grinned. 'You're quite safe. There won't be any shooting!'

Andre grinned back. 'A silly question, sorry.'

'You're not having second thoughts?' A humorous smile played at the corner of Rick's mouth.'

'Not at all. I like the idea of working for someone who is backed by the Union of All Nations.'

'You're right. We do have connections with the UAN, but the farm really stands alone in what it does for people.'

Quite suddenly it dawned on Andre. 'You're the mentor who paid my surgery fee…it was huge!'

'Yes. I hope…I hope you won't disappoint me.'

'Why would I do that when you've done so much for me?' Andre said, yet he hesitated when Rick put a pen in his hand to sign himself on.

'What is it?' Rick nodded at the truck driver who opened the door of the cab and made room for Andre.

'Nothing, nothing at all,' Andre replied. Of course, this made sense. He quashed an inner voice that held him back and signed. A moment's hesitation and then he was climbing into the cab.

Dreamlike, the journey went on, hour upon hour, the vehicle

swaying and rocking through endless plantations of giant trees, a strong smell of eucalyptus in the air, the screeching of birds, the swishing of overhanging tea-trees that brushed the vehicle. It felt like a game of blind man's bluff.

At intervals along the way there were warnings of land mines left over from earlier wars, a reminder of what dangerous times the people of Westland had lived through. Yet Mum and Dad always made us feel safe, Andre thought.

After a steady climb, they came to the journey's end. In the valley below was a glint of bright water where a river meandered through the forest. Along the river on one side lay a patchwork of fields, a cluster of houses, a home orchard and paddocks where a dozen or so dairy cows grazed. A security guard waved the driver through, over a bridge and gateway on to the farm. The truck came to a stop beside a row of sleeping huts with gleaming solar caps.

'You've come home, Singer.' Rick put an arm round his shoulder. 'The farm will take care of you now.'

16

Leila: The Meeting Place

Why has the warm sand grown cold? In my dream I had fallen asleep by the river. Mum came with a lantern to show me the way home, but the lantern merged with the light of the moon and I found myself without food or water. I had let small children steal from me.

Cursing myself for being so foolish, I decided to find shelter away from the track but a shadowy figure was hovering over me. Then I heard a soft, 'Leila?'

'Jacob, oh Jacob, I thought somebody was going to kill me.'

'You're freezing.' He had his warm hands around mine and was helping me up. 'And I bet you haven't eaten today.'

'I forgot to eat, and now I have no food. 'Oh Jacob, let's walk to keep warm and I'll tell you what happened.'

'I knew you were in the city and I knew about your backpack being stolen.'

I didn't know how he knew or even wonder why. Jacob was here and that was all that mattered.

'I've been looking for you,' he said. 'I thought...I hoped Emily would be with you.'

'She has been with me until these last few weeks.' I told him about how we came to be in the same place, about Shoeboy and Alrica and finding shelter with Bess. I talked until I had no words left in me. And Jacob told me his own story.

A rescue worker had wanted him to go to work for a man who grew the deadly kanza weed, but he'd given them both the slip. Since then, he'd lived from day to day, sometimes receiving food in return for helping people who couldn't afford to go to the health clinic with their wounds and illnesses.

I remembered Emily's fever and her cry, 'Oh if only Jacob were here,' and felt a fresh surge of joy at his presence. We stepped up our pace. A few hours ago, I hadn't wanted to live, but with Jacob beside me everything felt lighter.

He told me with a chuckle, 'Our footsteps are doing a perfect two-four beat.' At this, I sang, softly at first, until Jacob joined in, and our voices grew louder until we were shouting.

I left, I left, I left my wife in Timber-roo
with fifty buks and a broken shoe
I thought it was right, right
Right for my country whoop-de-doo!
I left, I left, I left my man in Timber-roo
with gov'ment bread you couldn't chew
I thought it was right, right
Right for my county – whoop-de-doo!

I threw my hat in the air and laughed out loud, and then it occurred to me to ask, 'Hey Jacob, where are we going?'

'We're going to my place.'

'Then I hope it has a carpet woven with gold.'

'And a table set with fine china?'

'Hey, you didn't mention food. Bugger the fine china unless there's food.'

Jacob had his belongings hidden on a wooded hillside. We padded over a thick mat of pine and Sheoak branchlets until we came to a clearing.

'This is it,' Jacob said. He lit a piece of dry twig with a flint and steel, his fingers making a tiny glowing lampshade, and then he lit a citronella candle. The light fanned out.

'Jacob,' I said, 'you look such a weirdo with your hair sticking out on end.'

'Seen yourself lately?'

'I haven't brushed my hair for days, and I haven't washed since I swam in a mine pool. I must look a fright.'

'You still look like Leila.' His eyes searched my face. 'I thought…I'd never see you again….'

'Me too…I mean you.' I made a sound, something between a laugh and a sob, but I didn't want to give way. Not yet.

Jacob's eyes glistened oddly. His voice was low as he touched my cheek. 'I think we'd better eat.'

'That's all we seem to think about now.' I laughed softly. 'Eating and finding each other.'

'The food is on me tonight,' Jacob said. 'But first I have a present for you.'

'My backpack?'

'Good that you had your name splashed all over it. Some kids from our village saw those little thieves trying to trade with it. They'd taken the food but we managed to get the backpack. I knew you were up here somewhere and kept looking until I found you.'

We spread our swags on the ground and then Jacob handed me a bowl of lupin seed from a farmer. It had cost Jacob his last buk. We sprinkled some water onto the seed and in the warm circle of light, ate the softened granules. Talking things over, we agreed that while conditions were so rough, Emily was better off with Bess.

'But we'll send her a message,' I suggested. 'I know a woman who will arrange it for us.'

I lay on top of my swag with my boots on, too tired to crawl into it. Jacob covered me with his spare blanket and then blew out the candle.

'Jacob,' I said, 'I like your carpet and you have a lovely roof, but we should give this place a name.'

'It's the Meeting Place,' he said.

I woke to a clear fine day. Now that I had Jacob with me, finding Bonnie didn't seem so hard or impossible. With his blanket close to my face I watched him, a rounded hill inside his swag, a mop of thick brown hair, a side view of nose and chin, a hand resting. Not a man's hand, not quite a boy's. Healing hands, Mum had called them. If he'd been born in another time, to another family, he might have been studying to be a medical practitioner or a surgeon.

I lay in a still curve waiting for him to waken.

Word spread quickly among ferls and orphans. Within a day, Shoeboy turned up, complete with Mum's dilly-bag of seeds, telling me, 'I didn't want Alrica to get 'em, did I?'

'I thought I'd lost them…forever.' I could hardly speak for the rush of tears to my eyes, while Shoeboy sat on his haunches grinning as I checked out the seeds, feeling them with my fingers, testing them for any moisture that might have ruined them. Satisfied, I strapped them round me to fit snugly against my middle.

'Have you eaten today, Shoeboy?' I asked.

'I haven't eaten and I haven't got food but I got some dimma and kanza weed to trade with.'

'Well, you can take it somewhere else.' I shot my head up in fright. Long ago I had promised Mum and Dad I'd have nothing to do with mind-benders. Dad had told us they mucked up your brain. Besides, he was so strict with us, I wouldn't dare. But I was curious and I couldn't help wondering how much food the stuff would buy.

Shoeboy looked around. 'There's nobody else here is there? Is he all right?'

'You're safe with Jacob,' I said.

He opened the raw dimma – white granules in a phial, and then the kanza weed – a whole leaf, rolled up, a yellowish colour and soft to touch with a peculiarly warm smell.

'I got this from Alrica, but this is the last,' he said. 'Nobody believes me but I'm going to buy a goat. A real live goat from the bush, not a hybrid. They're tougher than hybrids. I'm going to call her Gloria after my old gran because she told me how to rear and milk a goat.'

'Sounds like a good idea,' I told him. 'Where can you buy one?'

'I thought I might hang out with you for a bit and see what happens.'

'If you want to hang out with us, get rid of that stuff.' To my own ears I sounded just like Dad. 'We don't want kops coming around here thinking we're ferls...I mean...you know what I mean, Shoeboy.'

We picked up bits of bark, wood, pine cones and pine needles and then made a sluggish camp fire, taking turns to blow on it. A puff of blue smoke billowed and then the pine needles caught. We soon had a good hot fire. The light flickered over our faces.

'Look!' Jacob cried, 'the pine cones are opening with the heat. We can eat the nuts.' It was something else we could eat or trade with, along with Sheoak apples in season. While Jacob cooked some whole grain rice for us in his cooking pot, Shoeboy and I scrounged for more pine cones. We placed them around the hot bed of fire and like flower petals, they opened.

In the days ahead, other homeless children straggled up the hill to join us. Some were from our village. We usually greeted each other with the question, 'Have you eaten today?'

Any orphans who agreed to share a fire or exchange food would seal the agreement by spitting on his or her own palm and with a loud 'smack' slap the palm of the other 'trader' while chanting so that all present might witness the deal. 'If this be a lie slit me throat and let me die.' It was a habit picked up from ferls.

I wanted to go on looking for Bonnie, so Jacob, Shoeboy and I took up our loads and headed south. We had been told there was a refuge for young children at Camp C.

'Why go to a disease-ridden hell-hole?' A boy asked us. He was one of many we met who were moving away from there.

'I'm looking for my little sister and I have to check out all the camps until I find her.'

'You'd have to be lucky,' he said. Even while he spoke I had one eye out for the strangers who passed. Surely one of them had seen Bonnie. If I saw a little girl, my heart leapt, as though in every young child's face I would find Bonnie's face. There wasn't a moment when some part of me expected to find her. But after travelling for days we came away from Camp C with nothing.

'I'm glad your little sister isn't here for her sake,' a woman in the refuge at Camp C told me. 'There's a shortage of clean water here. That's why there's so much sickness. Be sure to boil your drinking water and wash yourselves every day or you 'll get the scabies.'

'Hah!' Shoeboy scoffed. 'I gets the sniffles every time I wash.'

While I had been in the refuge looking for Bonnie Jacob had wandered away. Though it was unspoken between us, I knew what he was doing – heading for the UAN registry of children known to have died from the epidemics.

'No,' he told me simply. 'They all had names and Bonnie wasn't one of them.'

In the days ahead, we made our way back to the Meeting Place, but we spent most of our time looking for food. If we were lucky, farmers gave us damaged grain and sometimes fruit in exchange for a few hours of work. We traded or we searched for bush tucker, snaring rabbits and other animals.

Watching me struggle with a blunt knife, one day, Jacob handed me his own, saying 'Keep it.' He had no stomach for killing although I had seen him treat the foulest- smelling wound of a stranger. That was how the knife for which Huldah bargained came back to me. I held it in my hand, feeling the lethal edge of the blade. Hardly a paring knife, I thought.

'What is it?' Jacob asked.

'Nothing,' I murmured, but in that moment, I saw where I had come to and I looked ahead to where I might one day be. With a sinking heart, I knew the time had come for me to go on with my journey alone.

Some boys had told us about a farmer who wanted workers to pick his crop of grapes.

'He's paying in hard coinage,' Jacob said.

'What are we waiting for?' Shoeboy's eyes flashed from me to Jacob and back to me. Jacob wanted money in his pocket to go and see Emily, and Shoeboy wanted his goat.

'You and Shoeboy must sign up then,' I said. Though I knew the dangers of travelling alone, for me there was no choice. I had heard of a refuge at a place called "Three Rivers".

17

A Lonely Way

I left a message with the LIV woman to tell Jacob where I was heading. The road ran like a dark stream over the dun-coloured land. On either side of the road, the trees hunched into one another. As if to whisper the sad secrets of those who had passed. Already I missed Jacob and Shoeboy, but I knew it would be wrong to expect them to come with me. I told myself, you've been alone before. You can do it. Only count the next ten steps. Don't look to the end of the road or measure the way in between.

A cold wind blew raw against my face. I had developed a cough that had slowly grown worse. My throat felt sore, my chest tight. You can't get sick. Not here. Not now. I drove myself until the sky darkened. Shoeboy had traded a pair of his best shoes for a bag of grain and some precious jars of honey, enough to keep us all going for a little while. I ate wholemeal grain moistened with cold water then lay down to sleep, trying not to think of my fear, but of Jacob and the light moments we had shared.

I remembered a cornfield. The sun warm on our faces. I looked at him and said, 'We are hungry and this is food.'

He grinned and with Shoeboy following we ran through the tall plants like crazy things. We sunk our teeth into the sweet yellow cobs sucking out every last bit of juice, laughing and groaning with pleasure, until out of the blue came the owner, with two snarling dogs at his heels.

'You damned orphans of Morwena,' he roared. 'Bugger off! That corn is for my pigs. Get going or I'll sool my dogs onto ya.'

A mad scramble for the fence. We ran from him. We ran and ran and then we fell down laughing until the tears streamed down our faces. Shoeboy pulled out a pile of corn he'd stuffed into the big pockets of his cape and we had to listen to him tell the story over again, mimicking the farmer and us, and even the dogs.

We two lay on our backs looking at the sky and then we turned to each other and the world seemed to hold only Jacob and me. Jacob, oh Jacob, I promise we'll be together again. Soon I'll find Bonnie. Soon. Very soon.

A low rumble of thunder woke me. Lightning flashed and the sky burst open. Sickness and fear pressed against my throat. I must keep going or I'll die in this lonely place and I must not die. Not here. Not now.

Soaked to the skin, my breath wheezy, I came to a dismal old house, the only sign of life, a pair of dirty grey horses standing together in the yard, their necks folded over one another.

I crept onto the veranda away from the stinging rain and wind. As I huddled against it, the door gave way and I stumbled into the room. A rat scurried across the floor and my skin prickled. I turned to run but felt myself dragged to the floor. Two strong hands circled my throat. She must have seen me come. Broad shouldered, black eyed, towering over me.

'Are you from GRIM or the kops? Chin thrust out, eyes stormy, she poked at me, and then grabbed my wrists with rough fingers.

'If you brought those GRIM bast'ds or the kops with you, I'll have ya guts for sausages and my brothers will string you up.' She opened a door and screamed, 'Alfie! Bronco! Daemon! There's a girl here workin' for GRIM or maybe the kops.'

'But I'm not working for anybody.' My teeth chattered. 'I'm just a kid travelling by myself. I'm wet and tired and I'm sick. I didn't want to come here only I had to get out of the rain.'

'You're not with those bast'ds? Then why didn't you say so?' At this I huddled into myself. I wanted to shut out the sight of this wild girl and her brothers who were sure to be as awful as their sister. I wouldn't tell them anything.

'If you're not with GRIM or the kops, then you can be my best friend,' the girl went on and on. 'I always wanted a best friend so you can stay here forever. And I'll be your friend too, but if you try to go away, I'll kill you. I will! You better believe me!' Her fierce, mad face came close to mine.

Behind the girl came another face. A cockscomb in orange, a flash of gold rings in ears and nose, a boy of about fifteen.

'Givin' you trouble is she Lucy? Want me to fix her up so's she can't do no harm?' he asked.

At this the girl turned on her brother in a fury, scratching at him and kicking him.

'Ow…ow…what was that for, you little spitfire? Bronco, Daemon, Lucy kicked me!'

Lucy screamed, 'Alfie was going to hurt my best friend and if he does that, I'll skin him alive. I will! You leave my best friend alone.'

The two older brothers were the biggest men I had ever seen, with gleaming eyes and heavy brows like scars across their faces. One carried a deadly butcher's knife in a sheath at his waist. He leaned over me as if he were inspecting an animal before the slaughter but Lucy turned on him, kicking and screaming, 'Don't dare kill her! Don't dare kill her, I want to keep her!'

'She's one of them orphans of Morwena,' said the brother.

'It don't make no difference. I'll feed her and look after her. I will! I will!'

The man picked me up by the elbows. I closed my eyes almost

fainting with terror and then he set me on my feet and said quietly, 'Daemon! Go and fix the meat. Alfie! Fill the tub up with water and make it hot. And Alfie, you leave them girls alone. You got no shame.'

'I didn't do nothink', Alfie bawled. 'Lucy started screamin' at me.'

Lucy glared at Alfie. Taking my hand, she dragged me to a huge shed at the back of the old house. Here the glow from oil-burning lanterns melded with the flickering light of a huge log fire. I stared into the blue-white heat, into its heart. Over the fire great cauldrons bubbled and steamed.

Bronco cut off slabs of meat from the carcass of an animo-cow which hung on a hook from the ceiling. He dunked it into a bowl of yeasty smelling beer and threw it on a hot plate with an explosion of peppery fumes.

The two older brothers worked side by side, dressed in chest-huggers and black studded pants. The glowing fire lit up brawny arms and swarthy faces, making their fierce eyes even darker.

'Alfie, hurry up with that water will ya?' Daemon bellowed.

The boy carried steaming buckets to a curtained-off bathroom at one end of the shed. 'I'm going as fast as I bloody can,' he panted.

I gaped at a bath built for giants.

'We take it in turns,' Lucy explained. 'You get first shot because you're the visitor. But we're not allowed to waste no water here.' She handed me a huge chunk of soap scented with sharp smelling oils. 'I'll wait outside for you so's Alfie don't do no pervin'.'

'I never did no pervin'– never,' Alfie protested, 'Nor wanted to, well not much anyways.'

I stripped and lowered myself into the bath. The soapy water seeped into my pores, cleaning off layers of grime, leaving my skin rosy and tender. The pungent fumes opened my strained airways. I floated as I breathed in the steam.

The tightness in my chest loosened and I drifted. In a half-dream, everything became clear. People weave their webs, try to hold you and keep you or suddenly unravel the sticky strands to let you through.

One day I will make a story I thought: A story about a ferl who gave me shelter and the one whose hatred haunts my dreams. I will make a story about Alrica, an angel with eyes that can blind you; an angel who will poison you with dainty treats and sweet milky tea; Alrica, wolf woman who feeds on children. My heart raced, my body heat trapped inside me. Alrica the wolf woman had a hold of my throat. But surely, I had escaped in the night with my magic hat and Emily, sweet Emily, whose feet are too soft and pink for rough roads; Emily who stitches moccasins while I go on with my journey. The weaving of dreams…a child with no name…Jacob and Shoeboy…and Stefan who has gone on a journey to save the world. People and places.

Now I had come to this place where rejects live. Lucy, the little sister would surely strangle me, and the terrible brothers. How can I possibly trust them?

Don't be sick, an inner voice warned. Sickness will make you a prisoner. Sickness will make you drop your guard, take away your will. You must find Bonnie. You must. Andre, where are you brother? Why aren't you here to help me?'

18

Andre: Dark Valley

For Andre the world closed in. He worked for the farm. Owed money to the farm. Owed his life to the farm. No more queuing for food. No bargaining or begging. With him were other homeless kids, some not yet thirteen years old. Each day was mapped out for them with work and rest. The only break in the routine was when Rick returned from his business trips for the farm.

Rick came and went on silver wings.

Andre watched a tiny flash of light in the sky slowly take on the shape of a solar plane. Once, twice, it circled the property and then landed gently on the field. Rick emerged from the plane laughing and a cry went up, 'Rick, Rick, Rick.'

'It's okay,' shouted a ferl called Oona, a spiky-haired girl of twelve. 'He's not disappointed.' This was the signal for the others, who rushed out to meet Rick. In their work-stained clothes they jostled each other to be first to touch his hand. Among them Rick stood out in black moleskins, a white silk shirt with a jangle of good luck charms flashing silver and gold on his chest. Unable to resist, Oona reached out to a glinting charm.

Rick laughed aloud at her daring. When Rick was happy the kids didn't need to be sad. It meant the report from the farm had been good.

'Last week's harvest of leaf from the crop was a record,' Rick said. And Snow had reported that another record was on its way. There were cheers and smiles and the promise of a shindig with music and dancing in the courtyard between the long-huts where they all slept.

Yet behind the smiles, Andre sensed Rick was watching those who smiled back at him and those who did not. The man's gaze rested more than a few seconds on the twins, Abbie and Rebecca, whose faces puckered with worry. Two weeks had passed since they had disappointed him, but now Zara was intervening on their behalf, asking if the twins might work in the same field again and be billeted together at night. Since the separation, Abbie had suffered one of her night seizures with an episode of vomiting afterwards. She needed her sister.

When Rick was happy there wasn't any need for sadness. All three girls begged and he forgave.

'Weren't you silly ones – forgetting the rule of silence and going off like that? You must never put your sister in danger again, Rebecca.'

Rick had his special helpers to hand out platters of food, special treats to celebrate his homecoming. In his easy style, he led them in song:

Deep in the forest, gay gypsy chorus
Bright glowing camp fire leaping before us
No land to hold him, no law to mould him
Light-hearted gypsy, free days enfold him….

'No law to mould him. That's Rick,' Andre said, 'yet he's got us just where he wants us.'

'Only because he's so good to us.' Tristan thrust a plate of sugared fruit at him to make his point.

'I don't call what he did to Abbie and Rebecca good.'

'Hey Andre, you don't laugh enough…even Zara thinks you've

grown as sour and crusty as an old night scrounger…Rick's start-
ing a line dance. Why don't you try it?' Tristan wanted to drag him
along, but there was no way Andre could bring himself to become
part of the charade they were all playing out. Even the self-willed
Rebecca was going along with Rick, joining in the dance – proba-
bly to protect her sister.

The girls had done nothing wrong except to have some fun
without Rick in the role of puppeteer. With their dark hair flying
behind them they had clattered into the courtyard, singing at the
top of their voices because it was their birthday. They'd forgotten
Rick had called a special meeting.

One look from Rick was enough. A moment that should have
been one of shared laughter turned into an insane kind of silence
in which anything might happen. For nobody knew what sly pun-
ishment Rick would hand out when he was angry, nor when it
might occur.

Later that same night the two girls were brought back by Snow.
He'd found them walking along the boundary of the property with
swags on their backs, looking for a way out.

There were always reasons why the light-hearted gypsy they
knew as Rick became a tight-lipped stranger. Tristan would point
them out. It had rained the week before and the leaf takings were
low. Rick was in trouble with the farm's bosses. If the takings were
low, they accused him of cheating. Rick had one of his dreadful
headaches. Rebecca and Abbie should have known.

'Rick, Rick, Rick,' Zara chanted with the others and it felt more
like a betrayal than ever. At first Andre thought it would be enough
just to see her, but now the sight of her hurt him so much, he had
to look away.

Quietly, he headed towards the main entrance without any real
purpose except to clear his head and find some peace. The last rays
of the sun spread over the valley with a brush of gold but this
paradise was surrounded by razor wire. And in truth it was filled

with a slippery kind of darkness that you couldn't get your head around.

Andre understood something of this on the day he arrived. Jack, one of the workers keeping watch at the gate, filled him in. This was a state-owned property and the farm did grow a small quota of food for the UAN to distribute to the people but its main business was the deadly kanza weed, a new strain, even more addictive and lethal than the old.

'How else would the farm have the money to pay your surgeon's bill?' Jack had asked, with a quizzical look.

'I suppose I should be grateful,' Andre said.

Jack shrugged. 'The farm has its reputation to think about, doesn't it? It does good deeds. It grows food for the hungry.'

'Then why do I feel like I'm trapped?'

Jack had looked at Andre steadily. 'There are no official records of you kids ever having come here. Does that tell you anything?' Yet Jack had urged him to go along with Rick and not to rock the boat. 'For the time being, you'll have a roof over your head and you won't starve.'

'Is that why you're in the business, Jack?' Andre was curious.

'When I first came, yes, that's why I was here.' He hadn't said any more except to add, 'Stay in there for now, but I promise it won't be forever.'

Now weeks later, seeing Jack still manning the watchtower, Andre wondered how a lowly worker like him could promise anything. Yet the man's calm strength made you believe in him.

Jack greeted Andre with a raised hand. 'Sorry you haven't been given a pass, Andre. You weren't thinking of having a night out on the town?'

'And get myself booby trapped? I don't think so.'

They were silent as the kids' voices wafted over the fields – again the insistent, Rick, Rick, Rick.

'I can't understand why the kids go along with him.' Andre

shook his head. 'They're not dumb. Tristan is a smart kid. Zara is too. What is it with them?'

Jack's dark eyes focussed on the two neat lines of long-huts and the courtyard between. The deep boom-boom of Zara's drum quickened. 'What those kids believe has nothing to do with being smart or not smart. They are hungry for heart and soul food. That's the prize Rick dangles before them.'

Don't I know it? Andre had been so hungry for it; he'd been hooked into telling Rick his long-held dream of making songs for Voice of World and how hard it had been to convince his dad, the man of action that such a dream mattered. Rick listened so earnestly. He seemed to really understand, yet when Andre attempted to sing a new song at one of the meetings, he had been rigid and cold, telling him, 'Oh yes, but you have a long way to go, Andre. Even if you are called Singer. Let's stick with the songs we all know.'

'You should go back, Andre.' The concerned expression on Jack's face reminded him that walking away from Rick's party had its dangers.

Oh yes, better to go back and to go along with Rick like so many of the kids – or be like Huldah who survived and waited without drawing attention to himself by becoming involved in what should or shouldn't be.

Andre knew himself well enough to know that he could do neither. Yet, as he listened to the singing and dancing, there was a part of him that wanted to be there with the others.

19

Andre: In Kanza Fields

In the red soil of the valley, the kanza plants grew taller than a man. Long broad leaves sprouted from a thick central stem. Pickers moved down the rows with a snapping sound, a rush of movement, quickly, quickly.

Snow watched over the workers. From the beginning, Andre sensed a dumb kind of hatred in the man. It was a trick of Snow's to put a boot on the hand of a child as he or she reached for the low leaves at the bottom of the plant. It was supposed to be a joke but sometimes he would press until tears formed in the child's eyes and then move on with a laugh, saying, 'Can't you take a bit of harmless teasing?'

Andre took in the rhythm of the picking as Huldah and Tristan rapped out the words: Reach with your right hand…snap off the leaf…lay it on your left arm…reach with your right hand…. For a moment Tristan looked small and funny against the monster plants. He began to add words, naming the bits of Snow he'd snap off if only he could, until Huldah hissed a warning, 'Shut up, Tristan he's coming. If he hears you we're done for.'

A silence fell on them like a shadow and their hands moved faster as Snow passed.

'He knows how hard we work,' Tristan whispered, but I reckon he knows we do it for Rick, not him.'

'Tristan,' Huldah said, 'I'm working for gold buks and nothing more.'

'It isn't Rick's fault that Snow's such a bast'd,' Tristan said in defence of his idol. 'Snow was sent here by somebody higher up in the business.'

'Snow's a bully,' said Huldah, flatly.

The days slipped by. Usually Zara worked in the gardens, but one day Andre found her beside him, her arms outstretched to take his leaf.

'I'm your carrier today,' she told him. Her face and limbs were already stained with black juice from the weed, her clothes filthy, yet there was an aura around her. Like a bleeding gum tree, he thought, where resin hardens to become something shining and beautiful. Zara took the kanza leaves from him with a smile on her lips, but he might have been anybody. He wanted to say, hey, do you remember me? Do you remember anything?

In the afternoon they all came together to work in the kanza shed, threading the central stem of each leaf onto wire prongs arranged on two sides of metre-long sticks. For hours Snow urged them to hurry but when Rick appeared the pace quickened. 'There's Rick!' the call went up, a murmur from one to another until the whole team buzzed. Today they'd broken their own record. Rick was happy so they didn't need to be sad.

Andre was so weary that night, he slept before he'd eaten or even washed the kanza filth from his body. Tristan woke him later, urging him to join the others in the courtyard.

'I can't join in, the way I feel.' A net seemed to be closing over them all. 'I'm afraid,' he admitted. 'I'm afraid of what Rick will do when he's through with us.'

'What are you talking about? Rick will always take care of us.'

Andre turned away from the sight of Tristan's face, so full of trust and love for Rick. It made him feel more alone than ever, alone and unsure, a half blind would-be singer, stumbling in the dark without a destination.

One afternoon Snow went away on some business, one of the few times they'd been left alone. Working across from Zara in the shed, Andre's spirits fell as he watched her unthinking smile. *It shuts me out. It shuts out reason.* Savagely he pushed a kanza leaf onto a sharp prong of wire. I won't …I won't give way to Rick. His hands moved faster and faster as if to ward off some evil. For a second, he lost his rhythm and the sharp wire slipped over his thumb in a jagged tear.

'Andre!' Tristan rushed to his side, crying out as if his own hand had been cut. 'Oh…no…no.'

Stupidly, Andre stared at the bloody wound. At once Zara came with a cotton pad to stem the bleeding and it was as if the hurt didn't belong to him anymore. All he saw was Zara trying not to look at his face.

'Look at me, damn it,' Andre demanded. 'I'm scarred but I'm still me. But Zara, you're not you anymore. You're like somebody else. Can't we talk about things like we used to? Can't any of us talk about what we're doing here?'

'Hush, Snow will be back any minute,' Zara's frightened face went pale.

'Oh yes. We're all so afraid of Snow. Maybe that's another thing we should talk about…Snow and Rick, wonderful Rick, who's going to solve all of our problems.'

'Don't you dare say anything about Rick?' Zara's face flushed with anger. 'Where would any of us be without him?'

Andre's own face burned. 'You really think that what's going on here is okay?'

'People are free to do what they want. Nobody makes them use kanza.'

'I wasn't talking about using, but I will if you want me to. You think growing stuff like this is all right when the whole country is crying out for food? And have you thought about some of the things we get here, like soap and things like that? Why do we get so much of it?'

'Rick gets it. It doesn't matter where he gets it. I suppose he buys it. Rick has to make a living. You can't always choose the way you do it.'

'That's not the way you used to think. You're so dazzled by Rick you can't see who he really is. He has a way with people. He fools people. He fools himself. Maybe he believes his own lies. Or may he's so keen to be one of the big fish, he'll do anything, use anybody, to get what he wants.'

'You don't know what you're saying.' Zara's eyes glinted with anger. 'We have to believe in Rick. He picked me up when I was out of my mind. He found out about my family, about Tyke. He's looking for your sisters.'

'Rick finds the kids he can use. He talks a lot about finding our sisters and brothers, but does he do it? Does he want to? Wouldn't that be a nuisance for him, to have a lot of little kids on his doorstep?'

'Shut up, Andre! I don't want to hear you.' Angry tears welled in Zara's eyes making her face blotched and furious. 'I wish you'd never come here. We were happy here until you came. You think I haven't looked at you. I have looked at you. I have. You're so self-righteous. So damned good, you make me sick. But you're still here, aren't you? You're still eating Rick's food. If we can't believe in Rick, we have nothing.'

'We have ourselves,' Andre said. 'If we can grow kanza, we can grow food. We could even go busking in the towns. If we worked together we could live. But first we'd need to get out of here without being zap-shot or booby-trapped.'

'You're mad. Rick would never do such a thing. Those things are here to keep the law-breakers out.'

'Are they? Are they really? Did you ever stop to think that growing and selling kanza weed is against the law? That even if the country is a mess, there's a government and a law?'

She closed eyes and her mind against him, her small features set like stone.

'Wrap your own bloody hand.' As she stormed off, he thought, I've lost her, knowing in his heart that his words had scraped the crust of a deeper wound than his own and that she was bleeding too. How do you know what the truth is? Who do you trust? How do you stay an okay person or know what to do?

Huldah hissed at him, 'Now you've upset her. You've upset Zara.'

'Yes Huldah, and that upsets you but you don't care a ferl's crap about the truth.'

'Shut up, and leave things be. We're going to be paid after the harvest. We'll have gold buks in our pockets and we'll walk out of here.'

'You think the farm will let us?' Using his teeth and one hand Andre tried to fix a strip of cloth around his bleeding thumb. With the bitter green kanza taste on his tongue, the raw stink of weed on his skin, something in him gave. His head raged with a new song:

They're grinding us down

Grinding us down with the weed

Bleeding us, blinding us

Grinding us down with the weed….

'Here, give me that rag and put out your hand. You're making a hell of a mess of it.' Andre winced as Huldah splashed a crude antiseptic over the cut and pulled the gaping edges together tightly, saying, 'You should have been stitched up, but that'll have to do.'

That night, sitting with Tristan in the courtyard, Andre put his song to music. The sound came as a trickle, like water from a clogged stream.

'That's so good to hear,' Tristan said. 'It's time you played your guitar. I've told you, you don't laugh enough. You should try one of Rick's trip-pills. When I can't laugh, that's what Rick gives me. I'm the only one allowed in his house. I'm the only one who can massage his headache away. Rick says he can make me rich. He says musicians and singers will bring the people together. That's why he gets disappointed when we mess up. He reckons if we perform in the towns, people will come and they'll buy lots of trip-pills and kanza.'

'You're telling me Rick is giving you mind-benders? Tristan you'd better be careful. That stuff can muck you around.'

Tristan shrugged him off with a laugh. 'You sound just like your dad.'

'Don't...don't say that.' With a stab of sorrow and regret, Andre remembered taking Rick into his confidence about hs Dad. Dad who was a giant compared to Rick. Then, with all the rawness of his feelings in his throat, he gave voice to his song: They are grinding us down...grinding us down with the weed, bleeding us, blinding us.'

'You call that a tune?' Zara said, dryly. 'You call that a lyric?'

'I call it a tune for the tone deaf. I call it a lyric for the blind.'

There was a ripple of uneasy whispering and then Tristan giggled, 'Andre, that's funny coming from you with that patch on your eye.'

'Oh yes,' Andre flashed back, 'but what about those with two good eyes who refuse to see?'

Jack, who'd been sent down to their quarters to make sure they got to bed on time, snapped at them. 'There's work to be done in the morning. Get to bed quickly.' He took Andre aside. 'You can save your energy for the weed as you call it. We're curing kanza tonight and you're on duty as of now.'

The furnaces that fed the kilns with hot air, burned brightly in the darkness. With the lantern in his hand, Jack opened the door of a kiln where the kanza leaf hung like yellow rags in rows on wooden frames above huge hot pipes. He showed Andre how to measure and record the temperature of the kiln.

Together they began the hard labour of feeding great logs of wood to the twin furnaces of each kiln.

Tensing his back muscles, Andre heard the worn cloth of his chest-hugger give way. With a wry smile he ripped it away and fed it to the flames. Naked to the waist, he worked on, breathing heavily from the effort. Red beams from the fire licked Andre's skin. Looking down at his chest, he realised with a shock that he wasn't the skinny bag-o-bones kid he'd once been. He'd filled out and grown taller. More Dads' son than he'd ever imagined. But what about the Singer inside him?

When all furnaces were going well and the temperature readings steady they took a break.

'I think we need to talk about your protest song,' Jack said, handing him a brew of tea. 'I know Rick and everyone behind him better than you do, Andre, so don't stir the pot.'

'I'm supposed to let things roll along as they are?'

'For the time being, yes and don't think I like it any more than you do. But I know just how far Rick will go.'

'He uses Snow to keep us in line and then has the gall to keep up this charade of being the good guy.'

'Do you want more tea?' Jack topped up his cup without waiting for an answer. 'You know, Andre, on one level Rick believes he is the good guy but he expects to get what he wants, always. If he heard about your protest song he'd use Snow to punish you. But I'm not going to tell him about it and I don't think any of the kids will.'

'We're all orphans of Morwena, and we don't dob on each other, even at our worst.' Yet even as Andre said it, he felt the fragile threads of friendship and trust dissolving.

'Trust me,' Jack said. 'Wait for me and when the right time

comes I'll help you…now let's get back to the job on hand.'

For Jack the subject was closed while Andre was left with his own thoughts. When the right time comes, Jack had said, but when will that be? And what does Jack mean? Can I really trust him? Will I ever get out of this place? Bonnie…Leila…I can't even remember your faces.

20

Dark Waters

While Andre cured kanza weed, I coughed and wheezed through the nights. Steady rain poured down for days. Flood waters rose, drowning low-lying fields, cutting off roads. I was imprisoned by my fever, by driving rain, by Lucy who fed me soup and hot drinks, guarding me jealously.

'You don't have to thank Alfie for washing the clothes and bed linen. That's his job,' Lucy whined, sulky when the brothers paid any attention to me. Even Bronco and Daemon were chased away when they tried to check on me.

'Her fever is worse. We should cool her,' said Bronco.

'I can do it,' said Lucy.

Too sick to care, I coughed and heaved again. My life seemed unreal, like some weird other world, days and days in the big shed with a whirl of movement and billowing steam.

Lying hot and limp, I might ask, 'What are the brothers making today?'

'They're makin' their foul brew of beer,' Lucy might say.

Sometimes they worked at great cauldrons, adding caustic soda to animo-fat for soap making, or filling the air with the sour smell of cheese made from goat milk.

'Alfie, get goin' on those dishes,' the older brothers bellowed. 'Alfie, stoke up that fire.'

'Alfie, get the washing done. Nice and clean now! Alfie!'

The others scolded, while Alfie ran from daybreak until dusk fetching and carrying, hoisting up loads of wet washing to the ceiling to drip and steam above our heads.

Sometimes at night I heard a truck hissing steam.

'It's Bronco and Daemon,' Lucy said. 'They made that truck their selves. They're doing LIV work. It's secret work. I'm not supposed to tell nobody about it.'

I put my hand on my badge and puzzled on it for as long as my tired brain would let me. 'But what does it mean?' I persisted.

'It means living,' Alfie whispered in passing.

As soon as my fever went down, Lucy and I left the shed to sleep in a loft above the haystack. The nights were long and strangely peaceful with the coo-coo of pigeons in the rafters, the sound of Lucy's even breathing in the trundle bed beside me, the clean-smelling hay.

In between showers of rain the horses rubbed their noses against the shed walls, whinnying softly. I drifted in and out of sleep, ever watchful. So too was Lucy who snapped awake whenever I stirred.

'What are you doing? Where are you going? I'll kill you if you try to leave. My brothers won't stop me. They let me do whatever I like, so don't you dare run away.'

When she was sure I wasn't about to leave, Lucy took a softer tone and would beg me to tell her a story. I became the mother, telling her about the myths of our land, how my own mother's people came to the continent on a magic rope.

'More, more, tell me more,' Lucy begged.

At such times she became like a young child of five or six. She loved my own story about a clever and brave Hero-Lily. 'Nobody ever told me stories before. Keep going. And what happened then?

What did Hero-Lily do when she found herself in prison? And who was the awful witch who wanted to keep her a prisoner? And what was happening to the poor lost brother and the sweet little sister.'

'It's only a story. I don't want to tell it anymore.'

'Please tell me about your father then.'

'Oh, very well,' I said, tiredly. 'My father's people were carried to the shores of Westland by a wave. Not an ordinary wave for she was their mother with a heart and a name.'

'What name? What name?' Lucy cried.

'Morwena,' I said, and I turned my face to the wall.

'I never had a best friend before, Leila.' Lucy's voice trembled in the dark.

'I was like you once, Lucy; I wanted a best friend more than anything.'

'And did you find one? What's her name? Is she still your best friend? Do you like her better than me?'

'Hush now, Lucy,' I whispered, 'Go to sleep. She's still my friend, but having a best friend was different from what I thought. I have other friends. I have myself.'

'What do you mean? You must like somebody best.'

'I don't know; each one is different. I like 'em because I do.'

'Hey Leila, if you're an orphan of Morwena you haven't got a mum or a dad, right?'

'But I do have a mum and dad. They're always here in my head. My dad growls at me when I want to give up and my mum holds me when I'm scared.'

'I reckon you're mad, but I like hearing you talk.' Lucy went on to tell me about her own parents. 'My mum went away and she don't ever come back. My dad neither. He was put in the correction bin because he stole things. Bronco and Daemon were in the bin too, but they ran away. Now they hide from the kops and they sell stuff they make like beer and soap at the markets.'

I laughed sleepily, 'So now they're run-aways they don't steal things…so what about Alfie…why is he painted like a fancy bird?'

'Alfie went looking for Mum and he came back looking like that. We others laugh at him but he don't care. He wants to be who he is.' Lucy's tired voice came through the dark. 'Before she got sick of living in a shed with run-aways, our mum used to sing for us.'

'Hush now, Lucy,' I whispered. 'If you listen, you'll hear the wind singing.' I listened too, and I saw fields of grass, rippling in waves, like water, like the sea.

But I must not think of the sea, and especially of a mother wave that gave her children to the land and then snatched them back again.

'You sound so sad when you talk about the wind,' Lucy sniffed. 'It makes me want to cry like I do when you tell me about Hero-Lily and her little sister and her poor lost brother. Where is the poor lost brother, Leila?'

21

Shadows

For Andre, the net closed in. Tighter and tighter. One day he watched Zara's hand tremble as she pushed a kanza leaf onto a wire prong. Unhappiness shadowed her face. Like somebody old, she struggled to pick up a stick weighed down with leaf and almost fell.

'You shouldn't do that by yourself.' Andre steadied her, taking the load from her. He sensed something inside her breaking. She straightened her shoulders and picked up another pronged stick, ready to fill it with more leaf.

They stood awkwardly in the narrow passage separated by a jagged crisscross of wires, and Andre could do nothing but go on with his work as though nothing had changed. Looking on, Snow remained silent, but his pale eyes seemed to say, 'Watch your step or you'll be hurt.'

That night, Andre worked the late shift, relieving Jack at midnight. He worked alone, manhandling heavy logs for the furnaces. Red faced from the heat, his skin glistened with sweat. When he was satisfied with the fires, he checked the temperature of the kiln and then rested for a while on his swag.

Sitting cross-legged, he picked up his guitar and plucked at the strings, chasing words and ideas, wishing Zara were with him to pick up the beat with her drum. He remembered how the kids came from all round when they heard her drum. Maybe it could once again, be a way of bringing brothers and sisters together.

Thoughtfully he strummed a few notes of the evasive tune in his head, and then, feeling uneasy, he stopped. 'Is that you, Jack?' Andre's skin prickled. Somebody was there in the dark. Secretly watching.

A few tense moments and Snow slid into the rim of light. 'I ought to break that damned guitar of yours, Singer.' He was in an ugly mood.

Andre tried to appear calm. Carefully he put the instrument away and then stood up ready to go back to work, but his heart thumped in his chest and he sprang back when Snow blocked him.

The foreman leapt forward, coming within an inch of Andre's face to spit out his malice. 'Rick and I know what you're up to. You want to stir up the others and ruin everything we've worked for. And it wasn't Jack who told us about your one-man protest. Think they're your friends, do you? Think they'll stick by you, eh? Well, there's a mole in your camp. A person who tells Rick everything. We know you're trying to get the others to leave.'

'I asked them to think, that was all.'

'Lying mother-pup!' Snow backhanded him across the face and pushed him against the kiln wall.

If I had a knife I'd kill the bast'd. A surge of fire burned in Andre's belly. Using all his strength he pushed against Snow. Taken unawares, Snow stumbled backwards and, before he could stop himself, Andre went for him, wanting more than anything to destroy that smooth face. As he looked down, it wasn't only Snow he saw, but images of Rick, smiling and handsome, preying on kids who believed in him. The men were users.

He held Snow's head back with one hand and clenched his fist ready to strike, but something held him back. It wasn't fear of

Snow, but fear of himself and what he might do to this man. For they both knew in that instant that Andre was the stronger of the two.

Enraged, Snow cried, 'Hit me! Hit me, you mother-pup! You bloody Singer!'

'That would make me like you and you are as low as they come.'

Snow, on his feet again lunged towards Andre, but Jack, who'd heard the scuffle stood between them. Barrel-chested and solid. With a calm strength, Jack defused the moment, allowing Snow to save face by ordering Andre back to work, telling him, 'Get that pile of logs stacked and don't waste any more of the farm's time.'

With adrenalin still pumping in his blood, Andre carried out Jack's orders, working furiously until his energy was spent. He breathed in the sharp air. Above him the sky seemed so wide and high. He felt strangely free. Free of Snow and Rick and everything they stood for. Feeling unafraid and strangely detached – he heard Snow's angry threats and then Jack's quiet reply.

'The LIV people know the Singer is here, so don't even think about hurting him. If you do, they'll find out.'

'How will they find out…are you going to tell them?'

'I will if I have to because I'm not into maiming and murdering kids. But think about this – if the Union of All Nations or Voice of World came sniffing around here, I reckon GRIM will get you first. The farm doesn't want this place under scrutiny right now with the harvest so near and nor does Rick.'

'You're a loser,' Snow snarled. 'Just another one of Rick's lame dogs. Like those homeless kids. You're nothing. If nothing goes missing, who's going to miss it?'

'I may be nothing, but I'm making sense.'

'Maybe, but I'll get the Singer in the end…when Rick gives the word, he's mine.'

It was almost morning when Jack confronted Andre.

'So, there's a mole in your camp!'

'Snow's making it up.' Andre didn't want to believe it. He gazed steadily at Jack. 'We don't dob on each other, but how about you Jack?'

'No, Andre.' Jack gazed at him solemnly. 'But Snow was right about one thing. I was a loser when Rick found me.'

Jack stopped to pour them both a cup of soup from an earthenware pot and they moved into the arc of warmth thrown by the furnace. He spoke of the wife he'd lost in the Killer's wake and his only child, a boy of thirteen who died in one of the epidemics soon after. When Rick recruited Jack, he'd been zombied out on trip-pills. 'But he didn't give me back a life,' Jack said, 'He gave me a job in a dirty business that uses children.'

It had taken Jack a while to take it in or even care but then he got mad. And when he got over being mad, he had this idea of passing the love he felt for his own boy onto somebody else's child. One day Rick sent Jack with the farm's quota of fruit and vegetables to the Three Rivers by boat. Along the way, he met up with a LIV man called Daemon. It was unofficial, but he was there to see the produce really got to the kids who needed it.

'He was there to keep me honest,' Jack said. 'I learned to trust him and he learned to trust me. He has a brother called Bronco and we meet downstream from here. There's a bunch of us. A rough bunch but we care about kids and we help each other help kids. We get to know things the Union of All Nations and the kops don't know. Sometimes we work with them.'

Andre shifted uneasily, realising what dangerous stuff this was. 'If the farm got to know about this, Jack, I reckon you'd be a dead man.'

'I trust you not to tell them.'

'Why me? Why have you told me this, Jack?'

'Because you're Singer. Not everyone who sings gets that name.'

The work went on, ceaselessly until the last of the crop had been picked clean. The cured leaves were then baled into hemp bags, Steel needles flashed. Huldah stabbed the lip of a bag, pulling the edges together, making great loops with twine, talking about what this meant for them.

'Tristan, we'll be paid soon. We'll have gold buks in our pockets and we can be out of here.'

Tristan's eyes shifted and he murmured, 'We'll see…we'll see what happens.'

One morning the kids woke to the distinctive whoosh of Rick's solar plane, moving above them like a giant silver bird. They went outside and followed it with their eyes—a lazy arc in the sky gradually fading into the blue.

'He'll be back,' Tristan whispered. 'He promised me.'

The crop had been stacked ready to be taken away when the farm gave the order. Now they were confronted by Snow who set them to work to clear the spent plants. They worked their way through the crop, acre upon acre, pulling, stacking and burning as they went. Back-breaking, filthy work with the sting of smoke in their eyes and the smell impregnating their hair and skin.

'It's better without Rick,' spiky-haired Oona whispered, 'you don't have to be so careful.'

Abbie glanced at Jack and then said, 'I'm glad you said that, Oona. I thought…I thought I was the only one.'

'What do you think will happen about our pay, Huldah?' Oona asked.

'Rick says if I stay with the farm, he'll make me rich,' Huldah said.

'That's not what he said to me,' Abbie cried, indignantly. 'He told me we didn't need gold buks, that the farm gave us everything.'

'Sounds like him,' Rebecca said, darkly. 'He makes up a different story for each one of us.'

They worked for hours without any lunch break. By late afternoon they were hungry and complaining. Back at their quarters they were met by Snow who told them he'd paid up the cook.

'You cook for yourselves from now on and you'll know how well you've been looked after.'

Zara called after him, 'How can we cook without food?'

He waved a hand from his truck, at the same time, eyeing Andre maliciously. 'I'll have a man bring up some meat…sometime.'

A queer kind of silence crept over them. Some of the kids raided the orchard and they came back with wind fallen apples. They lay about on the grass outside the sleeping huts. With time on their hands, the day seemed cold.

A large framed boy from our village strutted about bullying the younger children.

'Without Snow and Rick to keep order, we should make up some rules,' he said. 'Yeah, and if you don't keep 'em you go on trial and if you're guilty you cop it sweet.'

Zara turned on him. 'Haven't we enough to think about without you turning into another bully like Snow?'

A whiff of winter in the air. They went to bed shivering and hungry.

In the middle of the night, Andre was wakened by a disturbed garbled cry. He crawled out of his swag and soon after Zara appeared with an oil lantern in her hand. They whispered together.

'It was Huldah, having a nightmare again,' Andre told her.

Zara put the lantern down and their own shadows flickered above them as they listened to the sound of the other boys breathing. Huldah turned in his sleep with a troubled moan and then his breath evened out.

'I'm like him.' Zara's full lips trembled. 'I dream about the wave. It comes over and over.' She was silent for a moment and then she whispered, 'Andre, sometimes I think it would have been better if we'd all been taken.'

'Don't…don't say that.'

'No matter which way I look at it, the future seems so dark. Andre, what is to become of us? What are we going to do?'

Looking down at her upturned face, at the outline of her small breasts beneath the thin cotton night-gown, he felt as if somebody were carefully scraping away the inside of his heart.

'Andre, you were right. If we don't get out of here, we'll lose who we are.'

'Yes,' Andre said. 'But we'll find a way.' Yet in that moment he thought, everything we had is gone.

Zara looked fretfully at the other boys. Tristan rolled over and burrowed more deeply into his swag. 'He's asleep and he wouldn't do anything to hurt us, but I'm so afraid. Rick is more dangerous than Snow; he doesn't just want to use us. He wants to own us.' She leaned against him and he held her, simply to comfort her at first but it was like rain on dry grass. They melted into each other and she murmured his name, 'Andre, Andre, when you needed me I wasn't there for you.'

'But you're here for me now. We're both here for each other. Or I couldn't bear to hold you like this, not now, not ever again.'

22

Leila: K'un, The Horse

I woke to the soft whinnying of horses and I knew something was going to happen soon. Lucy flicked on a light that one of her brothers had rigged up. She leaned over me shaking my shoulder. 'What are you saying? Who is Andre?'

'Andre is my brother. I never told you so how did you know about him?'

'He's the lost brother like the one in your story. That story is about you, isn't it?'

Lucy cried heartbroken sobs for the poor lost brother and the sweet little sister. 'It's not fair,' she declared. 'We ought to get Bronco and Daemon ...and Alfie, to cut the witch in two for what she done to poor Hero-Lily.'

But when morning came Lucy was sad and angry in turn. 'You want to go lookin' for 'em, don't you?'

Before I could answer her, her fierce face came within inches of mine. 'You think we're rubbish. Just any old crims living in a dirty great shed. You don't want to be my friend.' She burst into tears and threw herself into Alfie's arms. He soothed and petted her until she could smile again. But when her eyes lighted on me she fell into a rage.

'If you try to leave me, I'll tell Bronco and Daemon when they come back from the LIV business and they'll make you stay. You better believe me.'

In a sudden turn-around, Lucy yelled, 'If you're going, go! Go now!' In a fury, she rushed outside, slamming the shed door. It echoed in the enormous space but within minutes she was back again, threatening to kill me and Alfie in one if he let me go.

After the tirade, she stood at the open door and let out a loud whistle. At once one of the horses came trotting up and as if on cue, Lucy sat on the horse's head and was whisked on to its back.

For a moment or two, the horse pranced about while Lucy straightened herself and then they were tearing across the fields with Lucy yelling, 'Yeah…yeah…giddup…yeah….'

After the storm came silence. Lucy had been like a chain around my neck and I should have felt light but something nameless weighed on me. I tried to reason with myself. Shouldn't I feel lighter? Shouldn't I want to be gone from here? What's holding me back?

As if he knew what was going through my head, Alfie said, 'It's always hard leaving but if you want to go, go now…and quick.' He grabbed a great block of cheese off the shelf for me, a loaf of bread and a generous chunk of soap, all the while urging me to hurry.

'There's no knowing what our Lucy will do. She's mad as a wild dog when she has a mind to be.' His quick hands scooped up my clothes from the washing line, and then he rolled each item tightly before stuffing it into my backpack. Only once did he stop to stroke my hat and lay it on his cheek before handing it to me. 'Nice,' he said. 'It feels nice.'

'You're a good washer. You made it like new.' I put it on my head. 'My Mum made this hat for me.'

'It's lovely, but be quick,' he urged. 'Lucy will be back any minute now.' I threw on my cape and with Alfie leading, we headed towards the gate. Yet as I hurried past the hayshed with its rose-printed curtains, I felt sad and weepy inside at the thought of Lucy – crazy Lucy – sniffing tears through my stories one moment and flying in to a rage the next. But I must not think about Lucy, I told myself, I must look to the road ahead.

I shook hands with Alfie and told him the next time anyone yelled at him he should threaten to run away and start a washing business in Three Rivers.

'Oh no,' said Alfie, 'I couldn't leave my little sister.' I understood how he felt for in a strange way I found myself hanging back, hoping…for something.

As if in reply, Lucy let out another loud whistle and came pelting towards me on the horse's back. I gasped; the horse looked bigger somehow, and whiter than I remembered. It was coming straight at me.

'Lucy's really going to kill me,' I screamed.

'Whoa…whoa…' Lucy shouted and the horse pulled up, a thunderbolt with hooves digging into the ground to stop the momentum. Face flushed, dark eyes glistening, Lucy slipped from the snorting animal's back. She stood like a tightly held storm, her back stiff and straight, her eyes averted. 'You're never going to come back no more, I can tell.'

I realised then, I wanted Lucy to let me go. I wanted to say goodbye to her. 'I don't know if I'll be able to come back to you, but I'll be thinking of you because you and your brothers saved my life.'

'Alfie don't do much. Not as much as me.'

'I think Alfie does more than anyone. I think you'd all miss him very much if he went away.'

'Alfie wouldn't do that,' she said, sulkily.

'I could,' Alfie said, with a mischievous grin. 'I could start a washing business.'

With arms folded, Lucy fumed while I dug out a jar of honey

from my things. It was the only thing I had to give away. 'Try this on your porridge but share it with Alfie and help with the cheese making and the washing and everything.'

'He don't need help,' Lucy sniffed, 'but I'll give him some honey.' She went on sulking but before I'd taken a dozen steps she called out, 'Wait…you can take the horse.'

A flush crept over my face. I couldn't believe this crazy girl. 'But how shall I get him back to you?'

'Getting him back is easy,' Alfie said. 'Near Three Rivers you'll find a big clump of two headed grasstrees. Let him go there. A slap on the rump and he'll be off. But first take the bit out of his mouth and tighten up the chin strap of the halter.' Alfie shrugged. 'Keep the reins; they're just a bit of old rope.'

'Thanks. I could use it to draw a bucket of water from the river or a well,' I said. 'But do tell me…what is the horse's name?'

'He hasn't got a name. He's just a horse,' said Lucy.

'Well I'm going to call him K'un from a story Mum told me.'

'Tell me that story,' Lucy asked in a wheedling tone, 'come back home and tell me.'

'I can't go back, Lucy,' I said, 'but I can tell you about K'un. He was a kind of god that lived long, long ago. He turned himself into a magical horse and the horse held back the waters of chaos.'

'Tell me more,' Lucy whined. 'I want to know about chaos. What is it?'

'It's about things going bad. Anyway, K'un brings you luck. He keeps bad things away.'

'K'un, I like that name,' Alfie said.

But Lucy was silent and sad, and in a lightening flash I knew what she wanted from me. It was the mother in my head. An awful pity swelled inside me, but I couldn't show it or ease the ache I felt. 'I must go, Lucy.'

Alfie made a stirrup of his fingers. A gentle heave and I was seated, very high and queenly, resting on my belongings which fitted comfortably against the horse's broad beam.

At once Lucy stopped sulking to skip and bounce in a half run beside the horse, all the while complaining. 'You didn't finish the story of Hero-Lily. Did she find her little sister? What happened to the poor lost brother? How did it end?' said Lucy, sister of runaway-rejects, biting her lip, holding back tears.

I waved and then I turned the horse towards the blue haze ahead. I don't know how it ended Lucy…I don't know the ending.

23

Andre: A Passage

'It's Jack with food.' This time it was Tristan who woke Andre. There was a scramble for cooking places on the char-burners with Huldah calling out, 'Anyone want to trade for a third of my rations?'

'Me...me...me.' Half a dozen kids wanted more food and the trading began.

'What have you got?'

'A ball of twine.'

'Six live yabbies'

'A pocket knife.'

'A bottle of healing oil.'

'The oil gets it,' Huldah called.

For a day they were light-hearted. The day was warm. The girls washed and plaited one another's hair. The boys washed their clothes by hand, blowing soap bubbles and flicking one another with wet towels. Their clothes flapped like sails in the wind.

Andre discarded his eye patch. He made a new song. Zara was to remember him singing that same day, wearing his scars without shame. His blind eye burned brightly in his sun-browned face. The new lyric came easily and they all sang.

When the icy south wind blows
I hold her warm laugh in my hand
To weave a magic cloak for you
Like sunlight, to hold you safe
Like sunlight, to hold you safe

But in the days to follow the kids grew hungry – and angry. Rick had deserted them. There was nothing for them here except a sense of entrapment and failure.

'We should walk out of here,' Rebecca declared.

Some kids murmured a weak protest about how disappointed Rick would be if they walked out without saying goodbye, but they sounded unsure. Frightened. A young child wept and could not stop.

'Do shush up,' Rebecca cried.

Another one sighed. 'I want everything to be like it was when we first came here.'

'It was never good for me,' Abbie said.

Only Tristan and four other boys went on hoping and believing. They waited near Rick's landing field, searching the sky for some sign.

At lunch time the following day Snow came with barely enough food to go around. Wanting answers Huldah confronted him. 'Why no food and no pay? Rick said he'd pay us when the crop was picked.'

'You know Rick, he makes promises he can't deliver. He has another assignment and I'm in charge of you now.'

'We had an agreement,' Huldah insisted.

'Where's the agreement? You'd have starved without us. Half of you owed us big buks when you came here.'

Savagely, Huldah turned on Snow, 'No doubt you kept a tally of what we owed you. Since you raise it, I did too and none of us are in debt to you.'

'Yeah?' A hollow laugh from Snow. 'Show me your figures.'

Huldah pointed to his head and his hands. 'They're in here and here. An agreement is an agreement.'

Snow laughed derisively, his eyes sullen and dangerous. 'What you signed was no agreement. The UAN reps don't even know you're here. There's nothing official, you either go along with us or your dead.'

'Surely he's bluffing,' Zara said, as he strode away.

'He's not bluffing.' Huldah's eyes narrowed. 'Rick and company are controlled by GRIM. I suspected as much from the very beginning. Now I'm sure of it. They use Rick to suck us in. Now they'll keep us in with their razor wire and landmines. Did you see the zap-gun in his pocket? I reckon he'd think nothing of using it.'

'Why did you come here, cousin?' Andre asked Huldah when they were alone.

Huldah looked at him steadily. 'I came because I had to. Because Tristan would have come no matter what I said…and there was Zara.' His eyes glistened. 'She would have died in Camp A without me.'

'I know. I know that.' Andre felt something tug – a mixture of jealousy and pity.

They cooked and ate their food in silence. Zara had struggled to share it fairly among the squabbling kids, going without herself to make it go around. The pot was empty when Oona showed up.

'Where were you?' Zara said, irritably.

'Fishing for yabbies,' Oona mumbled, though she had nothing to show for it.

Zara's eyes welled with frustrated tears. 'Oh, why did you stay so long? You're always going missing. Poking about into places you shouldn't. We forgot about you and now you'll have nothing to eat until Snow chooses to give us more. I'm so tired of it all!'

Huldah and Andre exchanged a look. Oona wasn't muddy enough to have been in the dam. They waited for their chance and tackled her.

'I hope your catch was worth it,' Andre said.

At the same time, Huldah lifted the lid of her bucket to expose, not the mottled brownish yabbies from the dam, but the slim clawed crustaceans found in cold river water, already cooked and ready to be eaten.

With her urchin face rumpled with worry and her impossible spiky hair sticking out on end, the girl crumbled. 'I'm sorry…I'm sorry. Don't tell anybody…I won't do it again.'

'Do what? You little trickster.' Huldah's sombre face lit up with a transforming grin.

'I gets them from the river,' came the reply.

'We know you got them from the river, but how?'

The razor wire fence around the farm made it impossible to get to the river unless you went through the front gate under the eye of the armed man in the watchtower.

'I think you'd betters show us,' Andre said.

Taking care to cover her tracks with false leads, Oona took them to a hillside on the norther border of the property, to the ruin of an old homestead littered with junk. Below it was a dam fouled by cattle. The whole area was a tangle of nettles and berries, criss-crossed by the trails of native animals and hybrids gone feral.

Picking their way along one of the trails they saw a deeply rutted channel below the dam. It must have carried the overflow in the wet, but it ended abruptly in a shallow depression, now overgrown with long summer grass.

'The water must go somewhere, hey?' Oona grinned at them. 'Ever heard of a storm well?'

Covered with a metal grill, the storm well was hidden by tree branches placed there by Oona. They uncovered it and then pulled the grill clear. Inside the gaping well they found a man-sized storm drain made from sturdy karri logs.

Andre caught his breath and his skin prickled at the chill of wet earth – the narrowing darkness. They waded through ground seepage for about fifty metres to a cave-like opening, with maidenhair fern and peppermints hanging like a curtain.

Using water washed rocks as stepping stones; they followed the emerging stream to a saucer like depression that overlooked a shining sweep of water. It was hidden from the river proper by a strip of land, an island overgrown with trees with channels at either end.

Oona pointed to the island and then led them to a raft. Made of drums lashed to a wooden platform equipped with a punting pole, it wobbled as they stepped down onto it. It was still anchored to a tree by a rope, so it drifted and then carried them back to its resting place against the island bank.

Among the overhanging trees, they had a good view of the river. Everything was quiet with only the sound of birds in the nearby forest. The wind rippled the water. A flock of black ducks rose with a flash of emerald wings.

'Listen!' Huldah gripped Andre's wrist. The echo of voices over water and then a boat came from downstream. A skiff …sleek and silent. Propelled by wind, paddle or solar power, the light weight vessel bore the Voice of World logo on its side…VOW.

Snow and Jack manned the metal sail. A woman stood between them. Dressed in working gear, she and Snow carried zap-guns hooked to their belts. Snow shouted to the helmsman and the boat veered so close they might have reached out and touched its side.

Snow joked with the woman, asking her if she'd ever skinny dipped in icy river water. The woman laughed and then Jack, leaning over, looked straight into Andre's face with startled eyes. At once he called loudly, 'Submerged log ahead…veer to starboard.' The boat passed. The raft lifted, rocking in the wake of a wave.

'Hell's living!' Huldah swore under his breath. 'I thought we were gone. But how did they get a Voice of World boat?'

'Snow got it from somebody who stole it,' Oona said. 'They're going to take out the seats and strip it down, and then use it for selling their kanza weed.'

'How do you know all this?' Huldah stared at her incredulously.

'I seen him, didn't I? Two nights ago, Snow, Rick, and the man who got the boat – they talked plenty.'

'You mean you come here at night by yourself?' Andre cried.

'It's the best time to get crusties. I been doing it since I was little. My Mum taught me to do it blind 'cos she's a ferl and we know these things.' She showed them the traps she'd devised and a char-burner made from a drum and fitted with a pot for cooking the catch.

'I found heaps of stuff in the old ruin.'

A tiny girl, always bedraggled, easily forgettable, now the centre of attention. She clowned around, doing a fair imitation of Snow trying to impress the woman. They laughed in spite of themselves and Huldah was saying, almost to himself, 'Any one of us could handle that skiff.'

'Yes,' Andre murmured. 'We're children of the wave…Morwena…born with the sea in our veins.' He felt the electric pull of the water beneath him but was remembering that split-second exchange between Jack and him. It wasn't just surprise that passed between them, nor fear, but a decision.

24

The Vow

A week had passed since Oona had shown Andre and Huldah the way out. Now Huldah spoke to the others.

'You'll only have the food queues and your wits in Three Rivers,' he warned. 'So, think about what you're doing. Don't buy a third of somebody's rations just so you can overfill your bellies for a day.'

They nodded their heads. For their own safety they had only been told to be ready when the call came. This would be a leap of faith, yet even Tristan went along with every suggestion without protesting or questioning. Somehow it played on Andre's mind. It all felt too easy.

'Any questions? Any doubts?' Huldah asked, and they shook their heads. It was the height of the kanza season. A dangerous time on the river Jack warned, with bitter rivalry between gangs of buyers and sellers. The children might easily be caught in the crossfire.

'Won't you come with us, Jack?' Andre had pleaded.

'I can't...I'm sorry.' Jack sounded uncomfortable. 'I'm caught up with something. But I won't let you down. You'll have the VOW within days and a LIV man to help you on your way.'

Listening to the murmur of Huldah's voice as he spoke to the others, Andre tried to prepare himself for the ordeal ahead. Jack had come at supper time with fresh food and dry rations for the children's swags and he'd given the signal.

Uneasily, Andre realised that Rick was back. He had returned late without fanfare, disappearing quickly into the homestead. Andre turned away from the glow of Rick's lighted window. He preferred to think of the kids all safely aboard the Vow with the current pulling strongly.

Jack had suggested Andre should snatch a few hours' sleep before leaving and so he lay down but something worried him, a small voice in his subconscious wanting to be heard. When he did manage to doze off, it was only to dream of a giant spider weaving its web across a dark space.

At three in the morning the sky became faintly light with a sliver of moon overhead. Andre kept to the plan precisely. He walked quickly without using a torch, following the outline of a fence as a guide, stopping now and then to listen. Wind ruffled the grass. A nocturnal bird let out a deep-throated wook-wook. Nothing else stirred, except his own fear lapping at the edges of his mind.

By the time he reached the hillside Andre was sweating. Using his torch now, he put his guitar and his bulging swag in the greater darkness of the ruin. He checked the time. Three-thirty. For a tremulous moment he thought he heard a sound, like the fluttering of wings of a bird disturbed. He waited, holding his breath and then came the thumping of roos flicking past him – quick shadows in the night.

Taking care not to show himself as a possible target against the increasing light, Andre followed an animal trail to the storm well. Once inside he ran sure footed and lightly along the drain without a backward look. Within minutes he'd made it to the river where a low mist hung. The LIV man was already there with his punt.

Daemon's LIV medallion glinted silver on his broad chest. He invited Andre aboard, speaking in the rough dialect of his kind.

Propelling the craft, he worked against the swift current with ease, his dark brows drawn together in concentration. As they neared the farm's brightly lit dock, their pace slackened.

Daemon nosed the punt into the shadows along the bank, moving forward little by little beneath overhanging trees until they were under the dock itself. They waited and then came the slight tremor of footsteps on the timber above them. The lookout man walked along the landing, flashing a high-powered torch into the boatshed and then across the water along the shadowy banks.

The man returned. He stopped directly above them. Andre held his breath; grateful for the deep shadows of the dock's supporting structures. Beside him, sat Daemon, as large as a tree and as still.

The lookout man yawned noisily and Andre released his breath. He seemed to be doing nothing more than rolling himself a cigarette. The heady smell of kanza weed, slowly paced footsteps, the clip-cop of his feet on the metal stairs of the watchtower and they both let out a sigh.

The man never varied his routine, Jack had said. Now he would disappear into the warmth of the galley for a stolen sleep.

Exactly on target, the lights at the watchtower failed. A carefully planned blackout by Jack. Andre grinned in the darkness. Using a skeleton key, they entered the shed. With a practised hand, Daemon scuttled the farm's high-powered hydro-ski and before he was ready for it, Andre had the wheel of the VOW in his hands.

The craft moved through the water like a trusted friend. Using no other power but the current, it cut a clear path to the island. Andre steered to port, coming to rest fifteen minutes ahead of schedule.

A few words to Daemon who had followed in the punt and Andre was back in the storm drain. No longer afraid but elated.

Quickly and quietly he made his way up past the dam to retrieve his belongings. Reaching into the darkness, he was startled by heat radiating from a man.

The steely muzzle of a zap-gun cut into his cheek.

Snow yelled at him, 'Where? Where did you get to?'

Andre reeled from the first blow to his seeing eye, a tearing pain from something hard ramming into his chest, a knot of darkness. The madness that drove Snow came at him in all of its savagery. Time lost all meaning; the hurting went on and on, until Andre cried out from somewhere deep in his soul.

'Enough!'

For some reason the word spoken so forcefully brought a moment of sanity in which Andre was able to break free, but then came the deafening crack of a zap-gun fired at close range. He heard the roar of a wave in his head. Morwena, with soft arms, reaching out for him.

25

Leila: Drummer

Sitting astride K'un on the crest of a high hill, I was filled with anguish. Below me three rivers glinted like frosted spider webs against the darkness of the land. Slowly, red light from the rising sun spread to where the three rivers became one broad stream.

'These waters will go on flowing whatever becomes of us,' I murmured, 'Oh, Andre, where are you and where is Bonnie?'

Was this just one more false lead? What if I failed again, only to be stranded in an unknown place far away from Jacob?

An electric shudder passed through K'un's body, as if to remind me of what to do. '

Soon we have to part, old friend,' I whispered. K'un had carried me through the roughest country I'd ever seen, finding trails between towering rocks and steep ravines, crossing swamplands and listless, barren fields. He had a nose for water and sweet long grass and would always find us a safe resting place for the night. Yet while K'un munched on wild oats guided by his animal wisdom, I hoarded more than a third of each day's ration, even when I was famished, the less I ate the less I wanted to eat. It was my first mistake. A step into danger.

Now as we moved along a pathway leading to the outskirts of

the town, a faint warm wind from the east brought the sound of a beating drum, filling me with urgency. 'Go, K'un! Go!' I dug my heels into the horse's sides, driving him until his flank foamed with sweat – and then I saw his ears laid back and his eyes rolling.

'I'm so…so sorry, K'un.'

Ashamed for driving him so hard, I pulled him up to a steady clip-clopping of hooves on the earth and I spoke to him, stroking his neck, telling him what a truly magical horse he was and just how much I would miss him.

In this way we went on with the rhythm of the drum beating in my head and the sound of K'un's hooves on the wind. We came at last to the stand of double-headed grasstrees Alfie spoke of and where I had to release K'un. Finding an irrigation channel in a field, we both drank and he nibbled for a while on lush green grass. I undid the reins, took the bit out of his mouth and secured the bridle. A slap on the rump and he trotted away.

All day the beat of the drum pulled me. I didn't want to stop until I had found it, yet as I came closer to the town of Three Rivers, I couldn't tell where the sound came from. On the outskirts of the town people worked small plots of land. A woman threw me a black look from behind a fence and a straggle of little kids gave up a game of tag to taunt me, 'We want no ferls, nor orphans of Morwena here. You're all dirty thieves. How did you get that hat…hey? Did you steal it?'

I marched on with my head high. The town buzzed with traders and buyers but still the sound of the drum went on. While I wove in and out of the crowd looking for the drummer, I felt the eyes of somebody watching me. He was dressed like a night-scrounger and carried a tin as night scroungers do, but there was something different about him. Scroungers didn't disguise themselves with their hair spread over their faces like ferls did. I turned away uneasily.

The sound of the drum grew louder. I was closer, and I knew

that sound, that little half-beat, followed by a steady rolling boom-boom. Zara...Andre, you composed that together in our own village street. I know you are near.

The drummer stopped and I ran through the crowd, bending under the weight of my load. My eyes flashed from one person to another. A street musician sat in the dust singing in a low whisper. His eyes blanked over when I spoke to him. 'I don't know any drummer. Have you got trip-pills for a poor old singer? Anything at all?'

I hurried on. I'd forgotten the night-scrounger, but there he was again, glowering at me through his hair. I walked quickly and he followed. When I stopped, he stopped. When I walked, he walked. I stood near the trading cart of a woman selling oil lanterns.

'Be on your way, Missy, unless you're going to buy,' she hissed.

'On your way, Miss,' a kop echoed.

Nervously, I moved on, aware of the night-scrounger some twenty paces behind me. I looked for the kop but he shook a finger at me. 'On your way, Miss, we don't want thieves here.'

Angrily I called out, 'I'm not a thief.'

Though I tossed my head proudly, my heartbeat quickened. I dodged between trading carts, trying to shake off the scrounger, my eyes scanning the crowd. Surely there was somebody I could trust. I looked for a group of kids about my age and then I saw him.

'Tristan!' I threw myself into my cousin's arms. For a moment we were speechless and then we laughed, hugging each other again. 'Tristan, I'm so pleased to see you. You're so clean and you're wearing a silk shirt!'

'Did the night-scrounger scare you? He's a ferl, a bad one. Stay clear of him.'

'Forget him. I want to talk about us. Where've you been?' The questions tumbled out of me. 'Where's Andre? What about Huldah? And Zara? I heard her drum.'

From the beginning I knew something was wrong but I didn't want to believe it. Questions flicked through my mind. Why can't he tell me what he knows? How thin he is, how pale and nervous. Why won't he look at me?

'Tristan, what is it? Aren't you with Huldah?'

'I made him cry. I never saw my brother cry before. But when we got to Three Rivers, I had to go with Rick's man. I promised Rick. I didn't mean anyone to be hurt. How could I Snow would do what he did?'

Nothing he said made sense. He was offering me trip-pills, telling me I didn't laugh enough. Talking about a white bird that took you away, 'just like in Rick's solar plane'. We had come to an open warehouse where kids zombied out on the floor. A girl lay in her own filth. I gagged, pulling Tristan away.

I pleaded with him to come with me. 'We'll find the others. I know Zara is near. Surely Andre will be with her. Huldah, too…you know how much he worries about you.'

He backed away. 'I don't want to see Huldah. I made him cry.'

I tried again. 'Tristan, brothers make each other cry but they don't just walk away. Come with me. I can't leave you like this.'

'You don't understand. I want to be with Rick. His man is taking me to him. When the kops raided the farm, Rick got away. He's taking me and some other boys a long way from here. We get to ride in his plane.'

'I don't understand. What happened, Tristan?'

'I just wanted to see Rick one more time and when I saw his light I went to his house. I told him Andre had gone somewhere, and that we were going too. I didn't know Snow would follow Andre.'

'Something has happened to Andre.' I looked into his eyes, trying to pull him back, but I knew I'd lost him. 'Then tell me where

I can find him,' I said. 'You owe me that, surely.'

'You'll find the drummer in the town square,' he said.

In a kind of dream, I found the town square and at once Zara saw me.

'Your brother is alive and so is mine.' They were the first words she said to me. I knew there was more. We sat down in the dust and she explained that she was playing the drum to bring back her little brother. A friendly kop told her he'd been hiding in the bush, but he was as slippery as an eel.

'I know Tyke will come if he hears me.'

Slowly she told me her story and it was as if I was there with Zara and the others on the farm that promised them so much. I pictured them on the night of their escape: a long line of kids holding onto a rope they had spliced themselves from scraps of wool they found in the fields. It was Abbie's idea to weave as many knots as there were children into the rope – it was something to hang onto in the dark.

A ferl called Oona led them with Huldah by her side. Following behind, Zara kept reaching out for Tristan, sensing his deep distress. 'We are all here, Tristan,' she said, 'you'll be all right.'

They were almost at the storm well when they heard the faint whirring of Rick's solar plane overhead. Zara saw the first rays of sunlight glinting red on the wide wings and then came the sound of kop sirens. They all stopped in their tracks.

'They're raiding the farm,' Huldah had said. 'We're quite safe.' He led them through the passage to the river, where they were met, not by Andre as they had expected, but by Jack, white faced. Daemon had already lifted Andre into the boat.

'He's alive,' Jack said.

How much time had passed since the night of their escape? My mind couldn't take it in. I followed Zara through a noisy throng going about its business, as though it didn't matter that my brother had been badly beaten and almost blinded.

A hawker called out, 'Cooked animo-steaks for cash or candle-wax.' The spicy smell of seasoned meat mingled with blue smoke from a char-burner and the sweaty odour of people packed in close. Zara led me away from the settlement along a path near the river.

Even though years have passed, I can see it all, the sun lying low, a red disk slipping behind the trees, the creeping darkness and a thin spiral of mist on the river. It was a human flood zone where the orphans of Morwena had come together from across the land. Zara pointed to a three-sided construction made of timber scraps, facing north, out of the wind. Later, I remembered only dimly, a dark-eyed girl leaving with Zara as I entered the rough shelter.

When I said his name, he let out a startled cry and the sound went through me, a sharp pin driven into my heart. Scarred and beaten, was this really my brother? 'My God,' I asked. 'What have they done to him?'

Andre held me, trying to comfort me, telling me the blindness in his good eye would go when the swelling went down, and as for the other, you can see with one eye as well as with two once you get used to it and wasn't he dreamy to let somebody hit his seeing eye? He'd have to duck next time but he was tired and would I mind if he went to sleep for a bit?

'Sleep now, sleep,' I murmured softly. I stayed with him, my fingers on the pulse of his wrist, willing it to go on beating. My own heart raced in startled spurts until I felt Andre's pulse ease to a steady beat, his chest rising and falling in sleep, an even rhythm like the wash of waves.

I sat by his side as he slept. Surely the world had stopped spinning, yet when I went outside, our piece of earth had turned right away from the sun. I gazed at a cold, star-pricked sky.

I whispered, 'No,' to a bright Southern Cross and the two pointers which tried to tell me this was a night like any other. 'No, this is not a night like any other.'

I ran to the shining river and I saw the face of the cruel universe there. It wanted everything I had. I raged. Did you have to do this? Did you have to do this to my brother? You've taken Mum, Dad, Bonnie…what else do you want? What have I got to give you? Do you want the clothes I'm wearing? Have my hat. Take it. Take everything…bast'd.

I let out a cry like an animal in terrible pain.

'Leila!' Andre called out. 'Are you there? What have you done?'

'I've just thrown my hat in the river,' I said, in a tiny voice, then burst into tears. I went to Andre and lay down beside him, putting my arm around his waist. He patted me carefully so he wouldn't hurt his broken ribs, telling me what a silly dimbat I was to throw away the hat I loved and to stand near the riverbank to be eaten alive by mozzies.

When at last I had recovered enough to light a candle, I saw that somebody had draped a silk scarf over an old lump of wood to make a table.

'Does Zara…you know…live here?' I asked.

'Does that bother you, Leila?' He couldn't see me smiling. 'Now who's being a dimbat?' Yet as I spoke, I heard a child's voice inside me crying, 'He's my brother and I love him too, remember.'

I set up my swag and we talked until the early hours, speaking more honestly about our feelings than we ever had before. He told me how Snow had fallen on his zap-gun and killed himself.

'The blast knocked me out, but his frenzy stopped when I yelled, enough! Strange that a single word saved my life.' In a low voice he went on with his story and I saw the crisscross of lives: of Andre, Zara, Huldah. And Tristan who betrayed them.

'Tristan hurt himself more than he hurt me,' Andre said.

'Andre,' I cried, 'there's so much danger out there for kids like us. How can Bonnie possibly survive without us? Surely time is running out for her.'

26

Bonnie: A Tree

Tyke was the one who told me about the tree you called "Mother". He showed me where you sat, a place where the light came through a lace of green leaves.

That was after you were taken away from the refuge by the foster parents.

One day Bonnie and Tyke were told, 'These kind people are giving you a proper home.' The woman in charge thought they should be pleased and grateful. 'You must call them Father and Mother.' Her eyes took on the gleam of hard brown stones.

'We'll get gov'ment rations if we take on a couple of kids,' the husband said.

'You mustn't mention such things,' said the wife.

'Government rations,' said the woman with stone eyes, 'and a small allowance.'

'I could use a boy for the garden,' said the man.

'I simply adore children,' said the woman.

Tyke called them the angry man and the tired woman. On the way to the old timber mill where the children would live, the foster parents took them to a place that looked like a castle.

'This is a wheat silo,' said the man, 'but the guards are drunk and they won't be watching.'

They hid behind low scrubby bushes. Because he was small and nifty, Tyke was sent by the man to steal wheat. He slipped under the razor wire and came back with one heavy load and then another.

'I had to get the wheat from under a tarpaulin. It smelled like rotten garlic.' Tyke groaned and his stomach heaved.

'That's the gas, stupid,' the man hissed. 'They use it to kill the weevils. You should have watched the wind.'

'You never told me.'

'He's only eight.'

'Shut up woman.' The man slapped Tyke around the ears.

The Old Mill was a small settlement near a forest. A place where people made furniture before the Killer struck. A row of houses backed on to a watery wasteland where people now threw their rubbish.

'Boy! You can help me make a garden.' The man swore and shouted and broke a spade. 'Nothing will grow in my garden,' he yelled.

'Not even dock weed,' Tyke said softly, 'and that will even grow in a bog.'

Day after day the man shouted and raved. The very sight of Tyke brought out a rage in him.

'You kids stay out of my way,' he warned, and so they ran to the old cherry plum orchard that had gone wild. From the heart of the tree they called, Mother, Bonnie watched the other man. He wasn't angry like the foster-father. He grew turnips, berries and carrots. He sometimes muttered, 'I ought to get the LIV people onto that bast'd.'

Tyke showed Bonnie how to move her eyelashes in a certain way to make a green speckled world around the gardener. He showed her how to look at the end of her nose to turn the gardener into two. The game would surely make her forget her empty stomach and the insect bites that scarred her body.

When they couldn't get to the Mother tree in time, they ran to the broken and looted furniture factory with its sawdust and silence and round jagged saws like eyes.

'Where are you kids?' the man bellowed.

Bonnie held her hand over her mouth to hold in her scream. She waited until Tyke told her, 'He's gone. He's gone to Three Rivers for rations.' He thought they should go into the bush. 'I can find bush tucker there.' He went searching for lizards while Bonnie sat on the ground playing with a little circle of stones.

The day went on hour upon hour but Tyke did not come back to you, Bonnie.

Bonnie went back to the house, to the angry man who was drunk and the tired woman who whined, 'Where is the boy? If he's lost we'll be in trouble. The LIV people will call in the UAN and the kops.' She wept and cried, 'Oh I thought if I had some children to love me, things would be better.' She would write her pain and fear in staggering lines in the pages of her diary.

She tried to hold you close but she was the ice lady.

Bonnie ran to her quilt, away from the woman who wanted to be called Mother. She cried for Tyke. She rocked from side to side humming some song. Was it the song Mum and I used to sing to you, Bonnie?

Bonnie woke. She heard Tyke scream, 'No, you will not hit me again. Never, ever!' He ran into the night. The woman wailed and even the man was frightened. 'We must go away with the girl. We'll be in trouble with the kops. The LIV people will catch up with us.'

'We always have to move,' the woman cried.

As they left, Bonnie cried too, 'I want my quilt.'

'You can't have it. It's a filthy rag. Shut that child up, woman.'

Bonnie moved from place to place with the man and the woman until they moved to the dark house where the deaf white cat lived alone with its silence.

27

Leila: A Meeting

'**M**y kop friend knows Tyke is moving closer to the town,' Zara told me. 'They've seen his tracks. Soon, he'll come to me.'

I left her in the town square and went to the refuge for young children. The woman in charge looked at me with contempt. When I told her about Bonnie, recognition flickered across her face. I was sure she knew something.

'There is no child of that name here.'

'No child without a known name?'

'I can't give out information like that to just anybody.' Her eyes were hard as stone.

'I'm not just anybody. I'm Bonnie's sister and I need to find her.'

'You're one of those homeless kids who make nuisances of themselves.' She complained about bad children who ran away from foster homes, bad children who stole from hard-working, honest people.

'You don't know anything about us.' I fought back tears.

'You lot will know all about it when you're sent to a correction camp. There's going to be a public meeting.'

When I went back to Andre to tell him about my disappointment, I found Jack with him. He shook my hand.

You're the LIV man who helped Andre,' I said.

Jack wanted us to go to the public meeting.

'I'd like every orphan of Morwena there, and the homeless kids you've picked up on the way.'

'You expect Andre to go like he is?' I swallowed a lump in my throat. Andre had recovered a little of his sight but his face was still swollen and bruised, his broken ribs a constant source of pain. It would take him weeks to recover from Snow's bashing.

'Why would any of us go to hear people insult us?' Tears scalded my eyes. 'Who will speak for us?'

From far away I heard the bleating of a true wild goat, a hawker's mournful call, the boom-boom of Zara's drum and between us, a troubled silence.

'We'll speak for ourselves.' Andre's voice was sure and even.

Jack's eyes glittered. 'We'll carry him if we have to.' He put an arm on Andre's shoulder. 'You won't be alone, Singer.'

It was the strangest meeting, with the strong whiff of carbide lamps that lit the darkness. So many faces, old and young, the orphans sitting cross legged on the ground in untidy rows.

I felt a ripple of uneasiness at our presence. This wasn't a meeting for us. It was a meeting about us. Words zigzagged down the rows of people.

'It's the LIV people mollycoddling them. Who ever heard of streeks, and even ferls, coming along to have their say?'

'Some of the kids are orphans of Morwena.'

'It makes no difference – orphans, ferls, does it matter what you call them?'

'Hush now, the Controller is going to talk. She's from our own government.'

'It's about time we did things for ourselves without the UAN and Voice of World.'

'We'll be voting for our own leaders soon. That's what this is really about.'

The controller smiled toothily, telling us about complaints from honest people. Slowly her eyes ran over us. The kids gazed at her stonily as she went on about people in the marketplace, farmers and hard-working families. They were angry.

'Some of you are stealing and trespassing. We do have rules. We have laws. If you don't keep them, then you'll be taken to a correction camp, and you wouldn't like that.'

A small boy with an old man's face spoke up. 'Any proper food in them places?'

'What's your name, boy?' the Controller asked.

'Me name is Salty,' he said.

'Well, Salty, if you're one of the orphans who ran away from a good foster home, you'll end up in one of those places and then you'll know.'

There were other speakers. Nobody knew what to do with us.

'There aren't enough gold buks in the government coffers to build correction camps,' a man grumbled.

A dull argument went on between the man and the Controller until Jack lost patience. Angrily he told how it was: about food rations getting lost, about people who hurt us and used us, about foster homes that weren't good at all. 'When are we going to help these children?'

Grumbles from the crowd.

'We can't look after our own families.'

'It's hard for all of us.'

A woman's angry voice. 'That's no excuse for food rations being stolen. The cheats and the ones who hurt these kids are the criminals. They're the ones who should be in correction camps.'

'Yes,' another woman agreed, 'and there should be a safe place for homeless kids.'

A government man calmed the woman. 'That's why I'm here.

I've had talks with the LIV people. We've agreed to provide a proper camp.'

'Will there be loo pits with tissues?' Salty piped up, 'cos gum leaves is scratchy.'

The kids giggled. Zara hushed them and then went up to the dais to speak. 'If we go into a camp, we need the right to trade; we need to come into the towns freely and to work for our living.'

My hands, my whole body shook but I knew I had to speak. When Zara had finished I jumped up on the dais. 'We need to be told the truth about our sisters and brothers. I'm looking for my little sister and the person at the refuge won't tell me anything about the small children whose names have been lost.'

Mutters of 'Shame' from the crowd. 'It's not right.'

The government man held up his hand. 'We can't get the Voice of World team right now, but give me six months and all records will be up to date.'

Six months! It was too long for Bonnie. I went back to my place, sitting down with my head in my hands. I wanted to weep. A hand touched my shoulder. It was Jack. 'Leila, look at our next speaker.'

He was sitting in the centre of the dais with his guitar leaning against his body, his fingers plucking the strings. Andre, no. Don't do it. I pleaded silently. Somebody muttered that the Controller had made protest songs illegal and should enforce the law.

I started to shake, while Jack, who had helped Andre onto the dais, now calmly sat down next to me. Like one of us. But you are not one of us.

'How could you let him do this? Do you want him locked up? Is that what you want?'

'Quiet!' A man called out. 'It's the Singer, rescued from Camp A.'

'I don't want to hear this.' I shook off Jack's hand.

'It's not what you think,' Jack said. 'Hush, Leila. Hush your lips and listen...listen to a real Singer.'

I'd never thought of my brother as a real singer. He was my brother who sang. My brother who used to drive me crazy with his tunes that wouldn't leave my head. But this was quite different. It came like pure spring water to quench a terrible thirst.

I'm reaching in the darkness

Reaching for your hand

Please don't leave me...

Leave me in the dark...

'That's what he sang when the rescue people found him,' the man said, while Jack murmured, 'Just look at the people all around. Neither Rick nor anyone from GRIM will dare touch him now.'

28

A Bracelet

After the meeting a woman came to me. She had worked in the refuge and knew of a small child who'd been given to a foster family from the Old Mill.

'A sad little girl. She wasn't able to speak.'

'Oh no, that doesn't sound like Bonnie. She speaks in proper sentences.' I went on about Bonnie, talking about her likes and dislikes. 'She's plump and she's really pretty,' I said.

The woman looked at me strangely. 'The Old Mill is only a day's walk from here. I think you should go and see. Please…come back to me if you want to know more.'

The next morning, I poured my heart out to Andre and for the first time I doubted myself.

'We have no proof that Bonnie is alive. What if I go there and find nothing?' Yet even as I spoke I pulled on my cape-jacket and picked up my swag, knowing there was only one thing to do, one place to go.

'Have you eaten today?' Andre asked.

'I have food in my backpack,' I said, as if that were proof that I wasn't slowly starving myself. 'What about you?'

'The other kids will look out for me.'

We spoke for a moment of living in a special camp for kids like us.

'I'd rather go back to Morwena,' Andre said. 'When we find Bonnie, let's do it.'

I heard the longing in his voice and I murmured, 'Of course,' yet, somehow, I couldn't see what he saw. I couldn't dream his dream. I was tired. If we go back to Morwena, I thought, we live with the sea and the sea is my enemy.

I touched his battered face. 'I'll see you tomorrow, brother,' I said, not daring to believe I would.

From far away I heard the thin high notes of Huldah's lip music. In the market place my older cousin pushed his trading cart. Dressed in an oversized cape-jacket and pants that flapped around his ankles, he leaned into the wind, stopping now and then to call, 'Healing oil for gold-buks or hydro-cells.'

I felt a pang at the sight of him – such a lonely scarecrow of a boy. He saw me and we stood face to face. I wanted more than anything to hug him but he held back from me and I didn't know how to breach the gap that held us apart.

'You're thinking about Tristan,' he said, 'and what happened to Andre because of him.' His eyes misted over. 'You blame me.'

'No, Huldah! Tristan made his own choice.'

'But somehow I let him down by just being who I am. Even now, after all that has happened, he'd rather be with Rick than with me.'

'Maybe I let him down. Maybe I should have tried harder to persuade him to come with me when I saw him. I don't know. I don't know anything anymore…as for Andre…he's a mess, isn't he?'

'Andre's not a mess and nor are you.' He flicked dust from the shelf of his trading cart and then said in his gruff way, 'I have something for you. It's Bonnie's name bracelet.'

I let out a sound – of surprise and fear – as he put it into my trembling hand. 'It scares me, Huldah,' I whispered. 'What does it mean?'

'That she has been in the Three Rivers refuge. A couple of volunteers had a racket going there. As kids came in for processing, anything made of gold went into their own swags. The stuff got hawked around the traders.'

'Oh Huldah, that means I'm close to finding her!' I felt like he'd given me a gift. I wanted to pay him. 'This must have cost you heaps.' I went on about the soap and cheese I could give him, talking too much as I do when I'm excited.

He threw me a look. 'Leila, I didn't ask to be paid. We're both children of Morwena aren't we?'

'Yes, and we're cousins.' I gave him the hug I wanted to give him in the first place. 'You bag of bones.' I grinned and he grinned back.

I fidgeted, making circles in the dust with my worn-out boot. 'Huldah,' I said. 'We should all stay together. You shouldn't be alone.' His eyes held mine for a moment and then, as I turned to go, he called out, 'Jacob and Emily came into town last night. They're with the ferl, the one they call Shoeboy.'

'Really!' My heart lifted.

'They're sleeping in the town square, the dagwits. Tell them I've fixed up a milking goat for 'em, but they're not my cousins.' He grinned. 'So, they'll have to pay me.'

Happily, I walked to the town square with Bonnie's bracelet in my hand. I imagined putting it on her wrist, my arms plump full with the feel of her. I'd throw her up in the air and catch her. More, more, she would cry.

In the town square I found Shoeboy curled up in his swag with his walkers neatly beside him. In a fit of mischief, I grabbed the shoes and stuffed them in my bag. Beside him, Jacob stirred and a little way along so did Emily.

I leaned over Jacob. 'Are you going to sleep forever?' I said.

He smiled sleepily, catching my hair in his hands. Clear grey eyes searched my face. Words fell from my lips about Huldah finding Bonnie's bracelet, about going out to the Old Mill to get her. 'I'll have her with me tomorrow,' I said.

Emily woke up and we exclaimed over one another. How long my hair had grown and how thin I'd become. How different she looked with her hair cut short.

I learned how Jacob and Shoeboy had persuaded her to come with them with promises of a life made easy with pure milk and cheese from a real wild goat. How they'd hitched a ride on a supply truck and how lonely it had been with just Bess and the baby.

By now Shoeboy was awake and yelling about a low-life thief who'd taken his shoes.

'Ah...so you agree it's a vile thing to steal somebody's shoes?'

'Leila! It were you.... Where are they?'

'If you want them, then catch me.' I made a flying leap over a sleeping ferl, brushing past two old night-scroungers sitting over a fire.

'Them kids got more energy than sense,' one grumbled.

'Shoeboy,' I yelled, 'What will you give me for the shoes?'

'My yellow teapot.'

'I don't want your yellow teapot, but I do want you to know what it's like to have your shoes taken and a promise never to do it again.'

'I can't say never ever....'

I threw one shoe and then the other as far as I could and he scrambled after them, muttering that he hardly ever did it anymore. He was helping Emily make moccasins and soon...soon he'd have his own real live goat.

When I had caught my breath, Jacob and Emily asked in turn, 'Have you eaten today?' They offered me heated wheatmeal.

'I don't need to eat.'

'And you don't need to snap our heads off,' Jacob said.

The energy spent in chasing Shoeboy had made me shaky, but I didn't want to swap food. If they gave me food, I'd have to give them some of mine and I wanted to save what I had in case I needed to buy my way to Bonnie.

When I told them about Huldah's offer Jacob said, 'How about we pick up the goat and then come with you?' He looked at me with a question in his eyes.

'You don't have to.' I didn't know why I was being so touchy and snappy with my best friends. I saw a flicker of hurt in Jacob's face but I couldn't take back my words or stop myself from slipping into the harness of my backpack. Stubbornness festered in me and it wouldn't see reason, for I was driven to go on alone.

29

Leila: Dream and Moonshine

I didn't look back. If I had, I might have seen another traveller slip into the bush beside the roadway.

My thoughts were on Bonnie. What if the foster family won't let me have her? I tried to imagine the moment of meeting, but I couldn't hold it in my mind.

Over hills and low swampy places, I trudged, while above me the white sky seemed to watch and wait. A cold wind cut through me. I pulled my cape close, missing my hat like a lost limb, something gone forever.

For hours on end, I went on, stopping now and then to eat a handful of moistened grain to ease the hollow feeling inside me. By the time I reached the Old Mill, the shadows had grown long. Coming into the street, I felt the eyes of people on me, but the settlement was veiled in a brooding silence. In a queer twist, it had been spared from the effects of the Killer, but there were no children's voices, nothing to lift the sense of desolation.

Timidly, I knocked on the door of one house and then another, but received no answers. At the third house a woman came to the door, her voice creaky and angry with fear. 'If you want a handout of food go somewhere else. If you want water, then get it from the bore like everybody else.'

When I explained why I had come she told me, 'Yes. There was…a bad family living next door with a boy and a little girl. The boy ran away and the others left. They left a feather quilt behind and it washed up real well, too.'

'Is it a quilt with yellow ducks, a blue sky and green grass?'

She blinked pale eyelids, her head tilted to one side like a displeased cocky.

'Please Mrs, that must be my sister's quilt. Can I buy it from you?' Quickly I took out some soap and a nice pat of goat cheese.

Little pinpoints of greed glinted in the woman's eyes. 'I reckon it'd be worth the soap and the cheese. It was filthy dirty when I found it and I had to use up quite a bit of my own soap. It took time and time's worth money too. You can't expect something for nothing. Not these days.'

With the quilt in my arms, I stood with my face buried in it as if that would bring Bonnie closer. All the while the woman whined about how hard she worked and didn't it show on her poor hands? But she was clean, she was indeed.

I let the woman's words ride over me. I was close, so close to finding Bonnie. In a daze I stumbled through the garden where the woman's husband worked.

'Want a few fresh turnips?' he asked.

The woman closed the flywire door with a sharp twang, while muttering about the husband giving away stuff he could easily sell, if only he had the sense.

'A married couple I know have a camp at one of the lakes,' he said. 'They've seen the people you're looking for. They're living in a house about twenty kilometres further on.' He told me to follow the forestry tracks, to be careful and to mind who I trusted. 'Enjoy the turnips.'

'Thank you…oh thank you.' I wanted to bite into the turnips right away…something crunchy and fresh from the ground, but I told myself, I need food to trade with. I need food for Bonnie.

Leaving the settlement, I found the track leading to the weir. The shadows grew long. The bush closed in. I pushed myself, trying not to think of my hunger and the biting cold. I didn't allow myself the smallest comfort. You have to keep going. You have to go on without stopping.

The snap of a twig, the crunch of a step on dry leaves, I jumped at the sound. 'Who's there?' My voice sounded hoarse and scared. I hurried on. Whoever it was, whatever it was, walked when I walked, ran when I ran. For a minute, I stopped to listen. Somebody else stopped with breath held, waiting.

I hurried through close overhanging bushes with prickles that scratched and tore at my face. A faint rustle of leaves, the dry snap of a footstep and again I ran, bending under the weight of my load, using up precious energy. I ran until I could run no more.

I shouted, 'Who are you? What are you?'

I grabbed Jacob's knife from within my swag and crouched on the ground. My head dropped low. Exhausted, my eyes closed for a second or two, perhaps longer, for I dreamed of a face, bony and ugly, with a mean drawn mouth. I forced myself awake.

From nearby came the yelp of a dog and then a man's voice. 'What's wrong with you, mate? Can you smell a fox? Calm down. No, you can't go hunting, stay at heel until we get to our camp.'

The little dog came into view followed by a man with dusky skin. He said, 'Hello. What are you doing here? Are you an orphan of Morwena?'

I don't know if I answered but he went on as though I had. 'Give me your load. Are you heading for the lake?' My wife and I are camped there. We'll give you a meal.'

I hesitated and then said, 'Thanks, I'd like that.'

As the sun set we came to the lake and my heart turned over

when I saw a little girl on the beach. I ran to her and I saw the softness of her brown skin, her chubby arms. Her eyes lit up as she ran past me into the arms of her father. I tried to explain to him why my voice thickened in my throat.

'It's just that I've been looking for my little sister for weeks and weeks.'

'It's all right.' The child's mother held me and told me not to cry and then changed her mind and said a cry would do me good and had I eaten today.

'No? I'll bet you haven't. Well, you're going to eat with us. We're having freshwater crusties and some special spuds my husband bought from the gardener at the Old Mill.'

I gave the woman the turnips and she steamed them with the central shoots left intact. The crustaceans were roasted with the shells on. How I craved food, yet when it was ready I couldn't eat. Miserably I lay down on my swag while the woman tucked me in. 'There's a hoarfrost tonight so keep warm. You can stay with us for as long as you like,' she whispered.

I fell asleep instantly and dreamed of a glossy animal with horns and a round-moon udder trickling steamy milk. When I awoke, the shining lake winked at me. A glazed moon smiled. It's perfectly safe. You'll find Bonnie quicker for your speed. Come now. Come now.

With liquid dream legs, I left the family who had been so kind to me, passing through swampland and forest to high country. Gradually the gentle mood of the night changed. The frosty air bit into my skin, chapping my bare legs until they oozed blood.

Across my path an owl flapped its great wings. An animal screamed. Fear chilled my soul. The stalker was near, dogging my footsteps, hurrying when I hurried, snapping twigs, swishing the long wet grass. I heard the echo of its sound, closer and closer. Felt it in the heaving of my breath, in the rushing of my blood.

Again, I grabbed Jacob's knife from my swag. Ahead of me was a pine plantation, a place where I could hide. But first I had to pass over a bare moonlit field. I ran, knowing the moment had come.

Halfway across the field I turned to see the stalker break cover. I sprinted away and almost made it to the forest, but he came at me in a flash. A brutish figure with matted hair, a pale face. Too quick. Too quick for a boy, or a man. In my soul I always knew he'd come after me.

From greed or hunger, the ferl made a dive for my swag first. I twisted my body, slipping the load from my shoulders. Bonnie's quilt is in there. Mum's seeds too, and food. Food for Bonnie.

Hot blood pounded in my head. I screamed at him, flashing Jacob's knife in an arc. 'I'm not a ferl like you!' In that instant, there was something in me, a creature more terrifying than any ferl, some deep vein which gave me the strength to keep what was mine. I fought off the predator until he was forced back – back, surprised and shocked by my fury.

The ferl they called Rattus, blundered into the scrub while I picked up my load and ran with wings on my heels, into the forest where the shadows lay in zebra stripes across the frozen ground.

From there, I could see the ferl, wolfing down some of the food that had fallen from my swag. For a while he prowled up and down screaming with rage. 'I never forget a face. I marked you, Leila Kieva. I marked you out long ago. Now you'll freeze. You'll know how it is for ferls.'

I don't care if I freeze. I'll never be a ferl. I 'll be a wild creature but never a ferl. I ran from his words, from his hatred. I ran from what I know people can be – but I knew I would live. Deep in the forest, I threw myself down on a thick mat of leaves and lay as still and closed as a pinecone guarding its seed.

30

Leila: Where the South Wind Blows

I huddled against the cold.

'I am safe here. I am safe here,' I whispered, but I dreamed of a bony hollow face. It was the stalker inside me. It was the face of hunger. I should have known.

I gulped down food, knowing I must eat, but my stomach turned to water. I had to clean myself on leaves. I whimpered, sometimes dropping to the ground with illness, but I forced myself on. I would find a road where people might see me. Good or bad, I had to take a chance. I needed somebody.

When I came to the road, I found a grasstree and set fire to the dry straw underneath the green. I watched the flames spark into the sky and then I slept. I was in a half dream when a man with a zap-gun in his hand looked down on me. 'Are you an orphan of Morwena? If you are, then what are you doing here?'

'I came to find a house. I'm looking for Bonnie...she's my sister...she's only little and she's not used to strangers...could you please tell me if you have seen her?'

I might have fallen asleep as I spoke to him. I might have

dreamed him. He didn't rob me or hurt me, but I knew something about him. 'You're afraid,' I said. 'You're afraid of me, and you know where Bonnie is.'

'I never hurt her...not that little one...I saved her...she kept running to the lake...where the waterweed looks like grass. You can ask my woman...I never did anything wrong.'

The man and his words became lost to me like a forgotten dream.

I have come for you Bihbi, I told her, I can feel your chubby arms round me, but why are you so cold? We are falling into a white dome. The world is upside down and Jacob is here. There's Jacob and Shoeboy and Emily too, her feet as brown and tough as my own.

A friendly circle of faces in the light of a citronella candle, but they are not smiling. Jacob knows. He knows my secret.

'You've been starving yourself. I knew you were in danger; that's why we followed you.'

Emily and Shoeboy scolded.

'You should have waited for us.'

'Lucky we met the people you camped with.'

'Lucky you lit the grasstree.'

'Have you eaten today?'

'You're frozen half to death.'

'Be careful how you warm her,' Jacob said. 'Do it slowly and don't rub her fingers or toes or she'll suffer a bad case of frostbite.'

They built up the fire with wood and pine cones, then warmed Bonnie's quilt, wrapping it around my feet. Jacob made a creamy gruel from oatmeal and goat milk, spooning it into my mouth, telling me that I must eat to live.

Afterwards I slept hour upon hour. Once I woke to find Jacob watching over me. He gave me a heated stone wrapped in a rabbit skin to warm my feet.

I said, 'I made a bad mistake. I might have put us all in danger.'

He said, 'You're safe now.'

Once I woke to find the animal of my dream smooching and nudging at the bedclothes. It wasn't a dream animal but Gloria, Shoeboy's goat; black and glistening. Her moon-round udder gave up three litres of milk each day to be drunk or made into cheese. She beat the ground with her little black hooves.

I woke again to find myself looking into Jacob's clear eyes.

'I went to the house,' he said. 'A man with a zap-gun chased me away. He thinks I'm a LIV person out to get him.'

31

The Ice Lady

Bihbi, little sister, the doors were barred; you were a prisoner in a house with a tangle of peppermint trees pushing under the eaves; dark creepers wound through cracks and broken windows.

The woman tells Bonnie the foster-father has left them. 'Now there is just you and me and the cat. You're my little girl. You must call me Mother. Why won't you call me mother?'

There are blue capsules amongst the woman's yellow vita-pills. 'You must never, never touch these capsules,' she warns. 'They are not for children. They will make you sleep forever.'

Peeping through the window, Bonnie sees the deaf white cat outside, arching its back, smiling a cat smile. She smiles at the cat. Without the man there will be a chance to run over the bright green grass and to find a sky in the golden lake where the sun waits with warm arms open.

The day grows dreary and dark. When the woman lets the cat in, it drags a half-eaten rabbit into the kitchen. They stand together looking at the cat, at the food in its mouth and then the woman hacks off boards from the wall with the axe. She lights a fire in the grate and feeds the flames with splinters of wood. The fuel crackles, the flames roar. The woman looks at it with glinting eyes as though she might eat the fire.

Bonne's stomach cramps with hunger as she waits for the meat to cook, but after the first warmth of the meal, the fire dies. The night creaks with darkness and cold. Water in the taps, turns to ice. The snapping air blows through the hole in the door where the foster-mother made a hole with the axe.

'Lie down. Lie down beside me,' she warns. 'Or you'll die of cold.'

Bihbi, you were afraid that if you lay with her, your blood would turn to ice.

Bonnie runs to another room, to a bundle of old rags that have been thrown into a corner for her. The cat curls up beside her giving comfort and warmth, away from the woman who wants to be called Mother. Bonnie, you didn't know I was so near.

Not far from the house, the four of us huddled together in a rough camp behind a covering of trees. The day before, we had skirted the lake where a wide fringe of waterweed grew like grass. Just above the surface, a rickety landing stretched towards the lake's centre…a glistening oval mirror that reflected back a pale wintery sky.

'The man goes shooting every morning,' Jacob said.

'Then we'll wait for him to leave the house before we go in for Bonnie.' I found a spot where I could go on looking for the man, but then, quite suddenly, after a burst of sunshine a hailstorm blew up and I had to take shelter under the groundsheet Jacob had set up for us all.

While the hail stones banked up around our ankles, we linked arms and chanted Hardie songs to charm the storm away. When it was over the sun broke from behind a cloud. The ground sparkled white. With bright eyes and rosy cheeks, Emily ran about, drunk with the strangeness of it, kicking up hailstones. Jacob made a ball of it and threw in the air. Emily caught it.

'Leila!'

I hardly heard for I was remembering the words of a stranger, words that haunted me for hours – ever since I saw the lake with its fringe of green.

Standing apart I heard the others shout.

'Got you in the back.'

'I owe you one.'

'Yeah and here it is.'

'Leila, what is it?' Jacob came to stand by me.

'Jacob! What a fool I've been. I thought I was remembering a dream, but I've seen the foster father. He had a zap-gun. He didn't threaten me…he wanted to tell me that he'd tried to protect Bonnie…that she kept wanting to go to the lake.' To see the upside-down sky. I started to run.

When Bonnie left the house, she must have seen the world as I saw it – the ground covered in a glitter of hailstones and, behind that, a shining lake where the sun flashed gold.

I found the imprint of Bonnie's body in the bundle of rags along with that of the white cat. In the kitchen, on the floor was a mush of spilled porridge – the work of a small child. It led me to the room where the woman lay, as if asleep but the hand lying above the quilt was lifeless and cold. The remainder of the capsules she had taken were scattered among vita-pills, face powders, coloured combs and broken beads – a broken life written in fragments in a book.

When the woman was a young girl she had lived in this house. She and her father had planted a garden in which blue roses grew, even in the heart of winter. In time I would read her story, but now I saw that this was Bonnie's story too, and so I snatched up the book jealously, slipping it into my pocket, and then I ran from the dark house, from the waxy whiteness of the woman's hand. I ran away from death.

I clattered over cobblestones, through a gnarled garden where blue rose petals had fallen and fantails flitted over the ground. I looked beyond to the dark swathe of Bonnie's tracks through the long, wet grass to the lake's edge. A flash of movement in the dark water and a turtle lifted its head, showing me a golden eye.

'No, no, no, you can't have her.' My throat closed over the words in my fear. Whimpering, I ran along the shore helplessly, for I was sure I'd lost her.

'Over there,' Jacob called from somewhere behind me, and for an unbelievable moment I saw her halfway across the landing that spanned the lake. A white brushstroke on a canvas of green. Like an egret, but the white bird of the marsh waits for its moment. She began to run.

I threw off my heavy cape and my boots and I bounded over gaps in the decaying timber beneath my feet, gaps through which a small child might easily fall. Slowly I gained on her and as I came closer I saw she had the cat in her arms. I slowed my pace, wary now, afraid of scaring her. To my little sister, I was just another stranger and she was so very tired of strangers. A quick glance at me and she turned her face towards the only way out, a place where the bright water gleamed, a white inverted dome, as soft and silent as snow.

I saw what she meant to do and I begged her, 'Bihbi…Bihbi, you're my sister.' At that moment the cat chose to wriggle out of her arms. I called softly, 'Come puss,' putting my hand in a movement that drew the animal to me. It was enough. As the cat padded towards me, Bonnie turned and I saw the look of recognition in her eyes.

My limbs were waterweed as I covered the space between us. I dropped to my knees, and you came close into my arms, burrowing your face into my shoulder. I held your frail little body. Close, oh so close. I smelled your hair, matted, unwashed, but still my Bihbi's hair.

The long, long search had ended but the little sister I once knew had gone forever. Now I must learn to love this child in a different way, I must learn to love in a different way. That in itself would be another journey, but now I mourned for all that had gone before, for the time when I was just a child myself with the feel and sound of the sea all around me. I heard it now, a song, wispy as the sound of wind in dry grass. I wanted to go home…back to Morwena, back to our land.

Let the warm tears flow, like a full river running into the sea. How it cuts, oh so deeply into the scarred earth.

Small birds darted around us, dipping into the water and then rising, dark curves, like leaves against the blue white air, and then Jacob, tall and loose-limbed came with Bonnie's quilt in his hand.

'You'll need this.' His damp eyes met mine and then he went back to the others. A small group near the lake's edge ready to meet us – precious friends who'd been with me in the dark.

They had my cape, boots and swag and were sharing my load between them so that Bonnie could ride high in my arms. Behind them Gloria nibbled on a clump of grass, her pink edged ears twitching. I made Bonnie snug inside her quilt, put on my boots and cape and then swung her onto my shoulders.

'Come Bihbi,' I said, 'we're going home to your brother.'

32

A Meeting Place

'Leila! Leila!' A rabble of little kids came running to meet me, brimming with questions.

'Was the LIV man in town?'

'Did you buy sugar cane?'

'Yes. Yes, to everything.' I knelt on the rough ground to make myself level with Bonnie, her small frame leaning against me. My mind flashed to the day on the lake three years ago. On that same day Tyke came in from the bush, his pockets bulging with sun baked lizards and bugs. We called him the Insect Collector. He stayed with us and taught Bonnie to smile and play like a child again.

Bonnie stroked my forearm. 'Andre told me we are having a meeting tomorrow. What's it all about?'

A tizz of excitement from the others.

'Are we going to another camp?'

'Tell us!' Tyke's dark possum eyes shone.

'Singer will tell you about it,' I said.

A raggedy little boy took his thumb out of his mouth to shout, 'Hoorah for Singer. We goin' to have a rave.'

More cries of joy as I dug deep into my bag.

'Look at the sugar cane!'

'Is it all for us?'

'Every bit of it,' I said.

The little ones sat cross-legged on the ground in a circle, chewing on the cane, talking, laughing, pointing at one another while I went on to our campsite at the foot of the hill. There were more than a hundred of us – raggled, taggled, living in our crude shelters, working our gardens, raising our animals.

As I passed, two boys whispered about me in low voices. 'She's called a meeting.'

'What's it all about?'

'I suppose Singer will tell us.'

My heart trembled. Conscious of eyes following me, I passed the camp, following a trail to the top on the hill. It was part of a range of hills overlooking Three Rivers township where I had sat astride Lucy's horse, K'un. Quietly I scaled the rocks to reach a flat slab of granite. Smooth. Sun warmed. A special place where a person might be alone to think. I made a small fire and sat cross-legged before it to stare into the flames. At the last show of hands, the kids had decided I should take a turn as leader. I had been quietly pleased but after seeing Jack, it weighed on me.

A month ago, there had been a great celebration in the town because Vesrigo and Nor'land had signed a peace treaty. The world had frightened itself with its own violence and vowed to end it.

We kids had been among the revellers along with streeks and ferls, dancing to the beat of every drum in Three Rivers, every singer, strummer and shaker. World peace…safety…fair trading between nations – these were the words on everybody's lips.

We can dream again, I thought. I picked Bonnie up and hugged her and then Jacob had his hand on my waist. We danced with the others in a circle. We danced with ourselves and each other. We kissed with melting lips. I shimmied as I hadn't done since the day I left Morwena.

Within days it came out. Vesrigo and Nor'land, two of the world's most powerful nations were hungry. They needed Westland's grain and would pay for it. The rice growers of Three Rivers saw this as their chance. Surveyors came into our camp with their measuring devices.

'What does this mean? Another move?' Rebecca asked worriedly. Nobody else said a word. Some of the kids used the surveying pegs for firewood.

'I've spoken to Jack,' Andre told me. 'I think you should do the same.' The LIV man had his own rooms now and could be found most days in Three Rivers.

'What were surveyors doing in our camp, Jack?' I asked him and without saying a word he put a map on the table in front of me. I was taken aback. I wanted to know about our camp and he was showing me a map of Westland. There were hard clear lines showing the various routes to Morwena. I had to avert my eyes from where the name stood out in bold letters because the dream Andre and I had about going back there had died. It had been declared a danger zone but lately there were rumours of a rebirth.

'Here in Three Rivers,' Jack said, 'the growers want the whole river basin for rice, a good enough idea in itself, but that includes your campsite.'

'But Jack, where does that leave us?' I stared at him blankly.

'The controller has suggested your old campsite.'

'Which one could that be?' I smiled a twisted smile, remembering the times we'd been moved on from place to place because somebody wanted the land or they just didn't want us – those damned orphans of Morwena and the rest, with their singing and drumming that went on into the night.

'They suggested the Fern Gully site,' Jack said, 'but I have another idea.'

Unwillingly my eyes went back to the map, to the picture symbols that spelled out things both helpful and unhelpful to travellers along the road to Morwena.

Jack's dark eyes challenged me. 'What's holding you back? Have you forgotten the dream you and Andre once had?'

'It's been too long.' I reminded him of the bitter winters we'd been through since then, the epidemics of sickness that had drained our will. 'We're settled now. Our gardens are coming on. The kids won't want to move.'

'They'll have to whether they like it or not. But it's more than that, Leila. Are you afraid…to take a chance?

'Of course,' I said. 'But I've been afraid before. You'd better tell me. What's the deal? Will there be land for us in Morwena? And will there be a place for the ferls?'

The fire on the rock burned low. The first chill of the night brushed my skin. The air stirred with sounds that marked the end of day: Shoeboy calling his goats for milking; the soft but powerful zoom-zoom of waterbirds flying home to their rookeries; Andre calling Bonnie to come in from her play; a straggle of kids coming back from the town, carrying their musical instruments if they'd been busking or dragging trading carts over the rough ground.

I watched some ferls skirting our camp. They disappeared into the wooded valley that separated us, then appeared again on the hill opposite. These were hard-core ferls, too savage and wild to want to live by our rules.

When the kops cracked down on GRIM, all the ferls had been dumped in our camp. Some stayed with us, to live in much the same way as we lived, but these others soon broke away to make their own dugout trenches and caves. Thanks to a boy named Salty, they made a living of sorts by growing edible mushrooms and a sour-tasting protein culture that thrived in the dark.

We had learned to rub along with the ferls, sharing the same drinking water, trading with them, warning them if we discovered the kops were on the lookout for those who were hunting and fishing on State land. The ferls were as tough as boots, but if they were sick or hurting, they'd send for Jacob.

I stirred the fire, smiling a little, remembering the ferl. One day Salty came into our camp looking frightened as he panted out his story. His camp had been hit with a rampant viro-bug.

'We're all deadly sick, but it's the Loner...he's come in from the bush and I think he's gonna die.'

We were huddled together in the long-hut. Rain had kept us locked inside for most of the day and so I welcomed the activity. I wasn't curious about who the Loner was. There were plenty of loners, living outside ferl law, but still connected in a loose way.

'Are you sure you want to come along?' Jacob asked. He exchanged a look with Andre that I didn't understand.

'Of course. Why wouldn't I come?' I often helped Jacob when he was treating sick kids. He'd taught me how to massage away aches and pains with the cleansing and healing creams he'd concocted from the leaves and seeds of eucalyptus trees and other plants with medicinal properties.

'Okay, you want to come.' Jacob shrugged and I followed him, not knowing what it was all about.

It might have been the narrow entry that scared me, but when we came to Salty's dugout, I swallowed my uneasiness. It opened out into quite a large room with a raised roof made from scraps of metal. Tallow lanterns flicked tongues of fire from small shelves cut into the earth walls. I took in a smoky animal smell mixed with the sharp scent of freshly laid pine needles on the floor.

Salty pointed to an inert pile of freshly cured skins...I guessed they were from animals poached by the ferls. It accounted for the meat that had been around in the markets.

From within the pile of skins there came a groan. Jacob threw the skins aside and I found myself staring into the face of Rattus. His feverish eyes locked on mine and he let out a hiss, like a wild native cat caught in a snare.

'Leila Kieva! Get her away from me...that crazy girl...get her away!' Overcome with a fit of coughing, his wheezy chest heaved and his colour darkened for want of air, but he went on gasping, 'Get her away!'

'Leila stays or I go,' Jacob said, in a firm calm way and then went on to chastise Salty and Rattus. 'Haven't I told you before how to treat a fever?' He threw back an enormous cape to expose the ferl's burning body curled up with six heated stones. 'Can't you get into your rat-eaten skull that too much heat will kill you?' Jacob cried.

Making a feeble lunge at one of the stones as Jacob removed them, the ferl's mouth opened and closed like a dying fish. 'You give me back them stones, you bugga...you just give 'em back.'

'Save your energy for breathing and stop your raving.' With these words Jacob shook something into the ferl's cup. My gaze leapt to his. I was shocked, for I was sure it was dimma he'd used.

'Sometimes it's all I can do,' he muttered. 'Can you see to him while I go to the others?'

His look told me: You insisted on coming, now make yourself useful and don't give me that look. But he gave me the option of having Salty stay with me.

'I'll be okay by myself,' I said, thankful for the reddish light thrown by the lanterns that covered my flaming cheeks. From my own medi-kit I took out a cooling cream that also acted as a cleanser, swabs of wool and a balm for the congestion. I arranged them neatly on a tray, lining them up like solders, while reminding myself that here was a boy just like another. He had a raging temperature and needed to be cooled.

Rattus flinched and I cringed but I went on, grimly intent on getting some of the grime off him. Using the cooling cream, I worked over him with downward strokes, ignoring his protesting grunts and his near nakedness. He was too sick to be concerned himself but as I worked on his legs towards his feet, he let out a yowl, crying, 'No…no…my feet are not for you to see Leila Kieva…leave my feet alone!' They were swathed in dirty rags fit only for incineration or burial.

'Oh, keep your feet to yourself then,' I muttered and then carried on with the job, for by now his skin was halfway to being clean. I poured the decongestant into my palms and worked on his torso with calm strokes. His protests slowly changed to a low croon and then he was silent. It may have been the effect of the dimma, but the anger and tension in his knotted muscles fell away.

I forgot who he was. He was a boy-man and he was very ill. When he fell asleep I covered him with the cape, putting just one heated stone wrapped in cloth at his feet.

Sitting cross-legged on the floor beside him, I nodded off to sleep. I woke with a start. Jacob had warned me and I knew what to do. The ferls temperature had soared again.

This time he didn't protest when I cooled him, but lay back to babble in a dialect I hardly understood but for the odd strong word. Suddenly in the midst of it all, the words he uttered became polished and clear.

I never spoke of the things he said, not even to Jacob.

In the days that followed our own camp was struck down by the same bug. It was weeks before we recovered. By the end of it, Bonnie was thin and listless. In despair, Andre and I thatched a nest for her from grass. Taking her out of the stuffy long-house, we carried her in the cradle to the hilltop from where she could see us working in the garden on the terrace below.

While she was confined in this way, Bonnie learned to read the sky. She watched the flight of birds, soon telling us which ones would be the next to fly above her, imitating their sounds, making their distinctive movements with her arms as though they were wings.

One day when the sun was high, an eagle appeared in an otherwise empty sky. Its enormous wings trembled above her. Bonnie had never seen such a bird before, but then suddenly in its place was a human face.

It looked down on her with strange burning eyes.

'So, you're the little sister,' said somebody with a hoarse whispery voice. 'I'm the Loner and here is my friend, Rattus.' Awestruck, Bonnie leapt up to take a closer look. A sleek bush rat leapt from the ferl's hand to his shoulder and then back again to his hand and then to the ground where it lay across a mangled pair of feet with half the toes missing.

Bonnie drew in her breath. 'Did your friend do that to you?' she whispered.

'Yes. Rattus bit off my toes. He did it all right,' said the ferl.

In our struggle to keep Bonnie healthy, I'd forgotten about the ferl, but when I saw him beside her my heart jolted with fright. I threw down my tools and ran, ready to fight him with my bare hands if I had to, but as I drew near, my quick distrust changed to something else.

He had his free hand up, in an attitude of surrender, saying, 'Back off, Leila Kieva…I didn't come to hurt this child…I came to give you and Jacob this.' He thrust a bark tray filled with mushrooms and protein culture into my hand and so I murmured a thank you. We stood in silence and then I said, 'Are going somewhere?' My gaze shifted to his back laden with gear.

At this he nodded and I bit my lip. 'I thought you might stay with Salty and the others….Better than being a loner don't you reckon? I mean…being a loner…must be…kind of lonely.' I gave an embarrassed kind of laugh. 'Salty said he'd let you stay….'

'Ahgh!' he muttered. 'Salty's a fussy bugga…he washes too much.'

'Why not make your own dugout nearby?'

'Ahgh! That's sugar-talk, Leila Kieva,' he grumbled. 'It's not for me. I've stayed too long already.'

'Go if you really want to, but before you do, I want to know your name so I can call you by it.'

For a moment I thought he was going to hit me and then he just looked at me.

'I'm not mocking you,' I said. 'I really want to know.' I put out my hands, the palms up, to make my point.

He stood mutely, then it came out creakily, like an old stone that had been embedded in the earth too long. 'My name…my name is Igor.'

'Igor,' I said, 'you won't believe this, but I do know what it's like for ferls. That's why I think you should stay with Salty.'

Something flicked across his face. Not quite a smile. 'I'm a loner,' he said. Then, with a faint saluting motion, he turned and disappeared into the scrub, hobbling along with his stick, surprising me with his speed and the quietness of his footsteps.

I recalled that moment when he had screamed at me, 'You'll freeze, Leila Kieva,' but it was he who'd been left with permanent scars from the night he stalked me. I wondered if he knew how much he told me in his delirium.

After we returned to Three Rivers with Bonnie, though he'd never spoken of it to me, Jacob had saved Igor's life by taking him to a medic who'd removed his frost-bitten toes. Perhaps it was because of Jacob that Igor lost his hatred of our kind.

Whether Igor found other ferls to live with, or whether he went chasing some dealer from GRIM to ease the pain of his cravings, I don't know, but I never saw him again. Remembering him as I sat by my fire, it was as though I were laying a ghost to rest, not Igor himself, but the deep revulsion and fear that he had once stirred in my soul.

That night, as the stars appeared in the sky, Zara beat her drum. From my place on the hill, I saw the kids surround Andre and I heard his words.

In honeyed coils the Tanjin River flows
Into the waters of Morwena
Morwena, our mother and our homeland,
Let us go back…back to Morwena

'Thank you, brother,' I whispered. With his music, Andre had reminded me again of where my heart belonged and, in his wisdom, he was preparing the others for our journey. At midnight one of the kids cried out in his sleep. A land breeze brushed our shelters as it rushed towards the sea. It seemed to me, not to be the wind, but some spirit, come to whisper and tease at our memories. My mind drifted…Morwena, our city, Morwena, the wave.

33

In Search of Sweet Water

I woke from a dream about a place under a forest of pines and Sheoaks. I remembered how bright the stars had been, how soft the pine needles and Sheoak branchlets under our swags. Jacob had called it the Meeting Place. It was there that Shoeboy had given me back Mum's dilly-bag of seeds.

I held the dilly-bag now, rolling the seeds gently with my palm through the cloth. Feeling Mum's presence, I told her, these seeds were raised from yours, Mum. I'm taking them home to our land.

In the morning I followed the path to the well. Already Huldah had a bucket brimming over. We filled our cups and drank.

'Here's to sweet water.' His dark eyes held a question. We had known all kinds of water, foul and fair. This was better than most, with the faintest earthy taste.

'The water in Morwena will be sweeter,' I said with a smile. 'You know it's time to go back.'

'The Singer seems to think so,' he murmured.

'I saw Jack yesterday. The growers want this campsite. They want us on that fern choked scrap of land way out past the town.'

'A hell-crap place to die.'

'A good reason not to go there.'

A troubled silence fell between us. 'Are you telling me it's the ferns or Morwena?'

'If we want any choice in the matter we move before the law is brought into it.'

'You mean the kops.'

No need for words, we both knew what that meant. If the growers wanted us out, we'd be forced into the other camp and not too gently.

Further down the hill, spirals of smoke rose from the cooking fires. They were illegal, but the kops let it go because we had no other fuel, except animo-dung when we could get it.

The kids stirred. Draped in skin capes and raggedy homespun pants, the little ones played a wild chasing game. They screamed as they ran up the hill with half a dozen goats bleating after them. We saw Bonnie trying to keep up on her skinny little legs.

'Can you imagine?' said Huldah, moodily. 'Going all the way to Morwena with this lot? How is Bonnie going to keep up?'

'Andre and I will carry her between us if we have to.'

'Will you carry Zara, too?'

He too, must have noticed the faint swelling of Zara's body, the soft look around her face and eyes. Huldah cast me a look.

I shrugged. 'These things happen. It will be a new life, something we should celebrate.'

His eyes misted over. Like me, he was remembering those who had been lost to us. 'I don't know if I want to go back without Tristan,' he said, softly. 'I've lost the only contact I had, so I don't even know where he is.'

'Speak with the ferls,' I said. 'There isn't much they don't know. And if he knows we are going back to Morwena, one day he might come back too.'

'Maybe I could do that, but what about the ferls? Are they going too?'

'I hope so. They have a nose for water and radar in their heads.

They can find their way in the dark like the blind.'

We stood in silence, taking in the sound of children's laughter and then the sound of Zara's drum slowly rising until that was all we heard. Huldah smiled crookedly and I smiled too. I wondered, will he ever stop loving her?

'Isn't it time you looked somewhere else?' I asked. 'There are other girls you know, I know one who really likes you.'

My cousin had lost his scarecrow look. He'd grown handsome in a dark way. 'We girls talk among ourselves about who we fancy. You know Rebecca? She reckons you're a babe.'

'Women!' He scowled, but his cheeks reddened. 'I mean…I never thought Rebecca would like me. What? What then? You're laughing at me.'

'No. I'd never laugh at you, Huldah.' I kicked the dirt with the toe of a worn shoe. 'But I know she'd be disappointed if you didn't come with us. And so would I. Huldah, we need a trader. Somebody we can trust who can work with the LIV people. We need you. Jack knows it and so does Andre.'

Huldah relaxed his shoulders and took in a lungful of air, as though he were letting go of something heavy.

'You'll come to the meeting to support me?'

'It looks like I'm already here. The meeting is coming to us, cousin. Even the ferls are here.' I snuck a look at him, at his eyes, bright with some thought of his own.

'I'm buying an animo-cart today…and…well…I had an idea. Bonnie could sit up on the cart when she tires.'

At the sound of Zara's drum, the little ones slid down the hill, giggling and shrieking. The others came from their fires in dribs and drabs. Bonnie streaked along the slope with the white cat with Tyke following. She jumped over a clump of grass before leaping into my arms. A moment to freeze.

'Leila, shut your eyes and open your mouth.' Her eyes shone with mischief and I noticed how plump her cheeks had become.

'Tyke has something for you,' she told me.

I shrieked. 'No way! I don't want any of Tyke's creepy-crawlies. What is it?'

'Purged snails,' Tyke said, eagerly. 'Try just a teeny one.'

Shoeboy was grappling with Gloria's latest offspring, but he stopped to tell me to try one of the snails. Them's are okay, Leila.'

'If them's are, then eat them yourself or give 'em to the goat.'

Behind Shoeboy came Jacob and Emily. My friend held out an offering. 'You'll need new moccasins if you're leading us home.'

'And you'll need a hat,' Jacob said. 'I found this one in the market.'

Somebody had stitched it by hand, using homespun cloth in dark blue, but Jacob had tucked an emerald feather from a black duck's wing in the band. Solemnly I slipped into my new moccasins and put the hat on my head, using Jacob's face as a mirror. He stood back, then tipped the hat to one side, ever so slightly towards my forehead. I didn't quite know whether to laugh or cry.

'Does this mean you both want to go back to Morwena?'

'Almost everyone wants to come.' Jacob stood with me, his fingers finding the soft side of my wrist. I knew in that moment that one day, we two would be joined under Hardie law in the tradition of our people. Just like you and dad, I told Mum, for I was sure she was near.

I felt snug in my new moccasins and taller in my hat, but before I spoke, I shook a little as I scanned the kids' faces. Their toughness told me, yes, we can make it. But they weren't easily pleased or persuaded.

'Are you goin' to get on with it?'

'What news have you got for us?'

Their wariness and fear were the same as mine, for we only had ourselves and a handful of people in LIV to support us. Jacob's hand on my wrist calmed me. I was able to tell them about the Controller's plan to send us to a fern choked camp where nothing else would grow. I reminded them of the last three years. So often we had planted seeds only to be moved on as our vegetables and berries ripened.

'Yeah and half the time we aren't allowed to sell our stuff,' a boy called out, 'because they reckon we're outsiders.'

I asked them how often they had heard, 'On your way orphans, you don't belong.' I searched their faces, 'Where do we belong?'

It came as a murmur and then more strongly. 'We belong in Morwena.'

'Yes. We are all children of Morwena,' I said. 'Morwena the wave, who claimed our parents. We have to forgive her and begin again.'

'Is it true that the lands our parents leased are going to be sold by the government to the highest bidder?' Huldah asked.

'They are going to try, but the law is on our side. If we are there, we can claim land for the group, enough to grow our gardens and keep our animals the way they should be kept. The LIV people have worked a deal so there will be room for you ferls to grow mushrooms and protein culture and to live the way you like to live. But the controllers in government don't expect us to make the journey. They don't expect us to know anything about the law.'

'You mean they'd rather have us rot in their fern choked camp.'

Everyone talked at once.

'It's not right.'

'We can't let them do this to us.'

'There is good black soil near the Tanjin River.'

'Would we be free to sell the stuff we grow?'

'Yes,' I said.

'Then let's vote.'

'Let's leave tomorrow.'

'It's such a long way to Morwena,' Emily looked at me with hope in her eyes. 'Can we do it?'

My mind flashed back over time and space. 'It's no further than any of us have already been.'

Busy days to throw away the things that would drag us down, to pick and dry the fruits of our gardens; to make biltong with the help of the ferls who came with meat after their mysterious nightly wanderings. The work brought us together but we needed something else and I knew just what we had to do.

We left in the late afternoon, stopping to make our first camp in a woodland where everlasting flowers grew. When we had made our preparations for that first night of our journey, I told the kids what was on my mind and a show of hands decided.

With quick sun burned hands we plucked the wild grasses along the wayside, binding the stems to weave our baskets. We filled them with sweet scented herbs and flowers. The next morning, I led the procession to the place where the three rivers merged into one. The light had come softly that day with feathery shadows and shafts of gold between the trees, a glint of red on the water.

Being the leader, I was the first to set mine free. 'To make peace with the sea,' I whispered, 'and to remember Mum and Dad and those others who were taken by the wave.'

Bonnie let her basket go and then cried because she'd lost her beautiful flowers. I comforted her by telling her we'd pick some more while the others set their baskets free. Shoeboy had woven some mohair into his for his gran, though she'd died long before the wave. Tyke put a chirping cricket and a dead butterfly in his for his mother. The ferls offered theirs for parents they'd never known or ones who had deserted them or treated them with cruelty. In that moment, all was forgiven.

Our tokens were picked up by the current.

So many dreams and wishes for what might have been, so many memories. Zara gave the signal with her drum. It was time to leave Three Rivers. While some had pushcarts, most of us carried our few belongings on our backs. We set off, the kids straggling one after the other. Already the younger ones were wasting energy by rushing ahead. Jacob called them back with a shrill whistle and they settled down.

I touched Andre's arm. 'Look at Bonnie,' I said. Clutching her flowers, she rode high in Huldah's animo-cart, with her eyes half closed against the wind.

'That's our Bihbi.' I sensed Andre pacing himself, fitting his stride to match Zara's and I wondered about the new song that was surely spinning around in his head.

Emily, who'd been walking ahead of me, turned to grin at me, and I remembered all we had been through together. We were different people now. I grinned back at her. Jacob who'd been chasing some of the kids for straying again, caught up with me. I felt his warm strong hand reaching for mine. Our footsteps worked a perfect two-four beat together.

We are the children of Morwena, I thought. I touched the dilly-bag of seeds at my waist. We have ridden a killer wave. We have our hands and these seeds and we're going home to our land.

THE END

Acknowledgements

Grateful thanks to artist Marion Duke for permission to use her original artwork. To novelist and independent publisher, Ian Andrew and graphic designer, Julie Rick from Leschenault Press. I appreciate your patience and generosity in the time you have spent in preparing this work to be accessed as an eBook and now as a paperback. Special thanks to Sarah Kempton for her magnificent work on the Audio Book version. Her skill in voicing the characters was stunning and the finished product is beautifully crafted.

My thanks also to earlier mentors, critics, readers, reviewers, Fremantle Press, friends and family who have encouraged me and believed in this story.

About the Author

Helene Smith was raised in a rural area at Linfarn Manjimup, Western Australia. Her school teacher mother handed on a love of literature and a tradition of storytelling which became a lifelong passion.

After a short nursing career, Helene married a school teacher and raised a large family, whilst all the time writing 'covertly' as a young mother – short fiction, private journal writing and poetry, honing her craft through TAFE correspondence courses. After studying Education and English and obtaining a degree as a mature student at Edith Cowan University in Bunbury, Western Australia, she wrote her first book; Operation Clancy (1994) was inspired by a wish to produce an 'easy to read' thriller for reluctant older readers.

Since then, the sheer joy of invention and a fascination with the writing process has kept Helene in there. An experienced presenter and writer/facilitator in schools, community centres and institutions for adult learners she delights in sharing the writing process with others.

Enjoyed the Book?
Leave a review

Follow Helene at http://helenesmith.com.au
Email: helene@helenesmith.com.au